Gold of the
Spirits

Don Kesterson

ISBN: 0998470716
ISBN 13: 9780998470719
Library of Congress Control Number: 2017903742
Amber Publishers Company, Parkersburg, WV

Chapter I

September 1, 1945

Manila, Philippines

TOM RAN HIS fingers over the gold-embossed letters on the cover of the black notebook: *United States of America - Federal Bureau of Investigations*. Only twenty-six hours ago, he'd lounged beside his pool—his parents' pool, actually—in the country whose name was emblazoned here. But now . . .

"Hanapin out!" The shout from the street below reminded him how far away from America he'd come. "Watch where you're going!"

Tom grinned. Traffic jam on the sidewalk. Some things were universal. He flipped open the cover of the notebook, still amazed to see his name and new title, *FBI Special Agent Thomas Paine Warren III - International Agent to the Philippines*, printed on the first page. What followed was practically a Bible; tabbed sections included an English-to-Tagalog dictionary he didn't need, a cultural guide, detailed maps of the islands and its cities, briefings on each of his two assistants— glorified bodyguards, Hoover called them—and most importantly, his mission. "My mission." The words felt more foreign on his tongue than anything he could speak in Tagalog.

Pounding on his door interrupted him. He glanced at his watch. The twelve-hour time difference still disoriented him, but at six-thirty in the evening, he wasn't expecting guests. Tom slid the notebook beneath the couch cushion, hustled to the door and slid the peephole cover to the side. The orbed, miniscule face peering back at him through the lens was anything but pleasant.

Tom smoothed his tie and opened the door. He recognized Edward Lansdale from Hoover's briefings. "Colonel Lansdale. Come in, sir."

Lansdale, in full US Air Force uniform, pushed past Tom. "I'm only going to say this once, Warren. This is my theater, my show. You may be on a mission from Hoover, but I run things in the Philippines, and no mission of yours will ever get in the way of what I'm doing here, understood?"

Tom licked his lips. "What mission?"

Lansdale poked him in the chest with his finger. "Don't play stupid with me. I know exactly why you're here."

"I don't think—"

"That's right. Don't think." Lansdale fixed him with a steely stare. "I do the thinking in the Philippines, got it? I know everything that goes on here. *Everything.*" The man's eyes roamed the room, found the half-empty glass of Jack Daniel's on the table, picked it up and downed it. He smoothed his mustache and glared at Tom. "Willoughby informed me of your so-called mission."

Willoughby. So that explained it. Willoughby was an old family friend, but he was Army, not FBI. Lansdale reported to Willoughby. Neither *should* have anything to do with Tom's mission.

"Like everyone else," Lansdale continued his rant. "Willoughby is in my pocket. *My* pocket. The Huks are in my pocket. The whole damn Philippine government is in my pocket. Am I clear?"

"That's a mighty big pocket, sir." Even as the words left his mouth, Tom regretted them.

Lansdale was in his face before Tom blinked. His nose nearly touched Tom's, and when he spoke through clenched teeth, Tom could not only smell the Jack on the man's breath, he could *taste* it. "Listen here, punk. I will strip you of your title and have you on a plane back to your daddy's house so fast what's left of your ass will touch ground before your feet do." He shoved Tom away from him. "Don't mess with me."

Tom sucked in a breath as Lansdale drove his shoulder hard into him as the man pushed past and stalked out the door, slamming it so hard behind him the watercolor print on the wall crashed to the floor. Tom stared at the door. He hadn't been on Philippine soil a full day, and he already had an enemy. Someone he'd assumed would be on his side.

He walked to the window, parted the curtain enough to watch the street below. In a moment, Lansdale exited the hotel and strode across the street to the edge of an alley, making a beeline toward a priest who stood in the shadows.

"What, he's going to ask absolution for nearly knocking me down?" Tom muttered.

The two men below him talked with their faces merely inches apart. Lansdale put his hand on the priest's shoulder and, in the last glimmer of evening sun, a palm-sized gold cross glinted on the priest's chest. Both men looked up at Tom's window, stone-faced.

Tom jumped backward, the hairs on his neck standing erect. Why were they staring at his room? *At him?*

Anger replaced his caution. He stepped back into the window frame and glared at them. *Let them see me. What are they going to do about it?*

But they were no longer interested in him. Lansdale and the priest separated, one going east and one going west. Who was the priest, and why had Lansdale obviously pointed Tom out to him? Tom touched the curtain just as a second loud pounding came at the door. His heart lurched.

This time, Tom reached into his briefcase, pulled out his pistol and stepped quietly to the door. He slid the peephole cover to the side, then slipped the gun into the back of his waistband. "McCoy," he said, opening the door.

Robert McCoy's eyes darted around the room. "Who the hell was just in here? Thought you'd been shot."

"If I had've, I'd have bled out by now." Tom scowled at his assistant. "Some bodyguard you are."

McCoy shrugged broad shoulders. "Hadda get my britches on."

Britches? Tom shook his head just as another knock came at the door. Before he could answer, the door swung open.

"You should keep your door locked at all times, boss. It isn't safe to leave it like this." Richard Love ran a hand through sun-bleached blond hair and cut a glance at McCoy. "You make that banging noise, Snake?"

McCoy glared at Ricky. "I done told you, don't call me that!"

Ricky squeezed around the large man and eyed Tom. "You okay, boss?"

Tom paced the living area of his hotel suite that wasn't consumed by his assistants. Finally, he stopped near them. "That noise you heard was Colonel Lansdale slamming the door."

"Ohhh." Snake's voice softened.

"What did you do to him?" Ricky asked.

Snake's eyes grew round. "Whatever it was, don't do it again. You don't want to mess with Edward Lansdale."

"How come?" Ricky asked.

"As long as I've been in the Philippines, he's been bad news. He's got a temper, that one. Snap his cap in an instant."

"How long have you been in the Philippines?" Tom asked.

"Long enough. Came back with MacArthur."

Tom turned to Ricky. "You?"

"Just got off the plane day before yesterday."

Tom frowned and resumed pacing. "What bothers me the most is that Hoover told me that only you two knew about our mission—that no one else in the Philippines—besides the FBI office, of course—even knew I'd arrived."

"Wellll," Snake drawled, "Willoughby's the one that gave me orders to work with you."

Tom stared at Snake. "Well, yeah, but I didn't think that counted."

"I don't know anything. Until he came and told me that you needed a driver and a bodyguard and that if I knew what was good for me, I should take the assignment."

"But that doesn't even make sense. Why would—"

"Nothing in the Philippines makes sense. Get used to it."

Tom looked at Ricky. "What about you? You Army?"

"No. FBI. Three years."

"Well, okay, then. I guess we'll meet tomorrow and go over our assignment."

Snake started for the door, then paused. "That Willoughby's another one I'd keep an eye on, if I was you."

Tom stopped pacing and stared at the man called *Snake*. "I've known Willoughby since I was a child. He and my father were close friends long before

I came into this world. He's the one—" He expelled a long breath. "I trust him. Let's leave it at that."

Snake held up calloused hands. "Whatever you say, boss. When're you gonna tell us about our mission? "

A dull ache swelled behind Tom's eyes, and he pinched the bridge of his nose. He'd wondered when his post-flight migraine would arrive, and it seemed it had just landed. "In a nutshell, we're to clean up the Philippines. Get rid of the Commies. The Philippines are gaining independence, and the US can't afford to let the Communists take over the country."

"Clean up the Philippines." Ricky barked out a harsh laugh. "Easy as pie."

Snake chuckled. "Yeah. You think? I've been here for a while. Nothing is as it seems—it's gonna be anything but easy."

The flat thud behind Tom's eyes pulsed rhythmically, and he squinted against the lamplight. He needed sleep. Desperately. "Look, gentlemen, I haven't shut my eyes in two days. Let's meet at the FBI office in the morning. We'll go over the assignment as I received it from Director Hoover. I'll fill you in on everything I know."

Ricky looked at Snake, who shrugged and loped toward the door. Ricky followed him out, then looked back and locked eyes with Tom. "Just be careful, boss. Okay?"

Tom locked the door after them, then sat on the edge of the bed and meticulously took off his shoes, then his suit, followed by his tie and shirt. Leaving on his socks and underwear, he lay on top of the perfectly made bed, doubling the pillow under his neck. Why would Hoover tell him that no one knew of their mission, then turn around and tell Willoughby about it? Did Lansdale really have Hoover in his pocket? And Willoughby, too?

He closed his eyes. Willoughby would never deceive him.

Chapter 2

September 2, 1945
Manila, Philippines

"Have you ever seen such a sight?" Tom stared at the circus-like party that filled the streets of Manila. He covered his ears and laughed as one of the trucks loaded with revelers blared its horn in celebration.

"*Digmaan Ang ay higit sa!*" a Filipino soldier shouted. "The war is over!" He grabbed the man next to him by the shoulders and shook him, and the two jumped up and down like little boys.

A mischievous grin curled Snake's full mouth, and he grabbed Ricky by the shoulders and shook him vigorously. "Hey, Ricky, the war is over!"

Ricky flung his arms, knocking Snake's hands from his shoulders. "Let go of me, you buffoon!" He straightened the lapel of his Hawaiian shirt and smoothed his too-long blond hair. He turned to Tom. "Can you believe we have to work with this idiot?"

Snake slid between the two men, clapping them both on the back before dropping his thick arms to his sides. "The pleasure's all yours, my friends."

Tom smiled and shook his head, too mesmerized by the festivities around him to get involved in the cloud of bickering that always surrounded his junior agents. Seemingly out of nowhere, pushcart vendors appeared in droves, hawking everything from sweet rice cakes, to *ukoy* shrimp patties, to orchids. Though it was early afternoon, liquor flowed, and men and women alike clinked bottles in toast to the war's end.

Not to be left out, Snake pulled out a flask from his hip pocket, took a long swig and passed it to Tom.

"Thanks." Tom swallowed a gulp, then let out a long, hot breath. "What is *that?*" He wiped his mouth on the back of his hand as his eyes watered.

Ricky hooted and mock-punched Snake on the shoulder. "You should have warned him."

Snake took the flask and passed it to Ricky, then offered Tom an innocent smile. "Homebrew, boss. Best moonshine the Carolinas ever made."

"Shine—you're kidding me. Where—when did you—how did you get that over here?"

Crinkles formed at the corners of Snake's eyes. "I got my ways."

Ricky took a slug from the flask and offered it to Tom. "Told you. He's a snake."

Tom held up a hand and shook his head. Snake took the flask from Ricky and shoved it into his hip pocket as the trio resumed meandering the streets, Tom a step behind his bodyguards. Again the continuous blaring horn, accompanied boisterous shouts, came from behind them. Tom turned to view the commotion, and that's when he saw her. His breathing stopped.

Perched atop the backrest of a beat-up convertible sat an auburn-haired beauty.

Tom stopped walking. He stood motionless as the river of festive people parted and flowed around him, continuing their celebration oblivious to his melting heart.

She wasn't that striking. One might say her fair skin and auburn hair was lovely in a classic sort of way, but she'd never be called breathtaking. Yet that was the very thing she did to Tom; she took away his breath.

A blur of activity swirled around him. Tom leaned forward to watch the redhead.

He walked faster, dodging in and out of the crowd in an effort to catch up to the woman on the car. Tom reached an intersection just in time to see the convertible turn down a side street, the woman atop it still gracing the crowd with a languid wave, as if she were a hometown American beauty queen. He darted in front of a slow-moving motorcycle with a sidecar, its Filipino passenger waving a huge American flag.

Tom jogged after the convertible, then slowed and smoothed back his hair and straightened his collar. The car had stopped and the woman stood in front of a street-vendor's cart. Tom's eyes roved her body. She was easily as tall as he was, and the skirt of her Navy uniform ended at two of the shapeliest calves he'd ever seen. The unbidden image of his hand caressing those legs caused his heart to race. What was it about this woman? He was Thomas Paine Warren III, known by his friends back home as the Romeo who could have any woman he wanted.

It was her boldness in sitting astride the convertible. Her confidence, apparent by the straightness of her posture and the tilt of her nose.

His palms felt sticky. He swiped them inside his pockets, then attempted a leisurely stroll in her direction. He willed his heart rate to slow as he mentally ran through the list of his most successful pick-up lines. None seemed to fit.

Tom reached her before he knew what he was going to say.

She looked up at him, her green eyes sparkling in the noonday sun. "Isn't it delightful?" She turned back to the vendor and waved away the handful of change he offered. "*Kumasta*. You keep it."

Tom licked his lips with a tongue like sandpaper. "Hi."

The woman laughed then, and it thrilled Tom that hers wasn't one of those high-pitched tinkles or trilling song-like giggles, but a hearty from-the-gut laugh. He smiled, and soon he was laughing with her, but had no idea why. "I'm Tom. Tom Warren. And I'm pleased to make your acquaintance." He held out his hand.

She smiled again, pulling her full lips into a wide smile that was a little lopsided. "But you haven't made my acquaintance, Tom Warren. You don't even know my name."

That was an invitation if he'd ever heard one. Tom pulled the woman into his arms and pressed a kiss onto those lips. He released her, half expecting to be slapped, but she only batted her eyes in surprise, then slowly, softly returned his kiss.

"Consider us acquainted," she said.

Ricky stepped toward them. "You know each other?"

Tom chuckled, then threw back his head and laughed.

The woman proffered a hand to Ricky. "Judith Ray. Pleased to meet you."

Ricky shook her hand, followed by Snake, who kissed it. "Ma'am. Good to make your acquaintance. Say you and Tom are friends?"

Judy's eyes danced when she looked at Tom, and he found himself laughing again. "Judith Ray." Tom rolled the name over his tongue. It felt good, like it belonged there. "Yes, you could say we're friends, at least." He offered his elbow, not the least bit surprised when Judith slipped a hand into the crook of his arm and stepped beside him. She waved to her friends.

"See ya back at the ship, Judy!" a woman hollered. The convertible took off.

She glanced at Snake, then Ricky. "So where are we off to, boys?"

Two hours, three bars, and at least half a dozen drinks later, Tom still hadn't been able to shake loose his bodyguards. "Why don't you guys head back?" he said. "Judith—*Judy*—and I will find our way later."

A broken neon light flashed near Ricky, casting an odd blue glow over his blond hair. "Our job is to protect you, and we aren't leaving you this time. Hell, with the streets full of partiers mixed with soldiers and rebels, we ought to have you squirreled away in your room, anyhow."

Tom threw back another shot and glared at the man, but Ricky's face blurred in front of him. The now-familiar thud resumed its drumbeat behind Tom's eyes. *No. Not another migraine. Not now.* He should've known better than to drink so much, especially on top of Snake's moonshine.

Judy held out a cigarette. Tom reached into his pocket and fumbled for matches.

Snake leaned between them, a blue and yellow flame flickering from his Zippo lighter.

Judy pursed her lips, took a long drag, tossed back her head and blew a slow line of blue smoke toward the ceiling. She leveled her gaze at Tom. "So what is it you do, Tom Warren? You never did say."

Tom tried to smile, but it felt like a grimace. "No, I didn't, did I?"

Judy laughed. "A mystery man." She held up a hand before Tom could speak again. "Don't tell me. I like mysteries. I'll figure it out eventually."

"Eventually." Tom liked the sound of that, even if the word did slur on his tongue.

Snake stood and downed what was left of his drink. "On to the next bar?"

"Sure!" Judy took a last drag from her cigarette before crushing it out in an ashtray.

"Sure," Tom echoed. He rose to his feet, nearly staggering as fresh pain bloomed behind his eyes. He stumbled over a crooked board in the old hardwood floor.

Ricky grabbed Tom's elbow. "Boss, you okay?"

Tom squinted at the man. "Migraine's back."

Ricky nodded solemnly and walked close to Tom as they headed for the exit. Snake held open the door, and Tom followed Judy out of the dark, smoky bar. The bright afternoon sun hit him like a bolt of lightning. He flung his arm up to protect his eyes from the sunlight and the pain, but it was too much. He staggered toward the side of the building as Ricky caught and steadied him.

"Whoa, there," Ricky said.

Judy instantly sobered and stepped toward Tom, putting her hand on his bowed head. "Hey, are you all right?"

Ricky shook his head. "Migraine. He spent a lot of time on an airplane and hasn't had much sleep."

"Oh, you poor, poor man." Judy's eyes scanned over Tom's face. "I'm a nurse." She pulled a handkerchief from between her breasts and dabbed Tom's forehead. Her eyes roamed from Snake to Ricky and back. "Get him home—wherever that is. Turn out the lights and pull the shades. He'll need the room as dark as you can get it. Place a damp cloth over his eyes. Put a pitcher of water and a wastebasket at his bedside."

Snake looked confused. "Wastebasket?"

Judy frowned at him. "He'll be sick soon. Get him home."

Snake stared at his boss, then looked at Ricky for guidance.

"Go now." Judy made scooting motions with her hands. "You hear me? Get him home before he vomits."

Tom covered his eyes and raised his head. An aura of light surrounded Judy's face, and despite the wave of nausea that accompanied the throb of pain in his temples, he realized he'd fallen for an angel.

Chapter 3

September 3, 1945
Manila, Philippines

TOM TURNED THE page and narrowed his eyes as he tried to read the hundred-page report Charles Willoughby had left for him at FBI headquarters. Even though Willoughby was Army, not FBI, he had a great deal of knowledge about the presence of Communist infiltration in the Philippines and had volunteered to present Tom with his findings—although Tom had no clue the "findings" would fill a hundred-page report.

He rubbed his temples. The conference room was stifling. The old rusted fan in the corner of the room no longer worked, so there was no airflow. To make matters worse, a state-of-the-art fluorescent light hung low, the long tube flickering to a rhythm of its own. Tom looked across the small conference table at Ricky. "You mind reading this to me?" He pinched the bridge of his nose and squinted. "At this rate, I'll never get through it before Willoughby gets here."

Ricky reached across the table and took the bound report. "Should we wait for Snake before we go on?"

"Where is he, anyway?" Pain throbbed with each word Tom spoke. "He should've been here by now."

"He swore he'd only be a few minutes. Said he had to take care of something."

Tom scowled. "Read."

Ricky cleared his throat. "The Hukbalahap obtained much-needed arms—"

"Just call them *Huks*, please. Easier to say, easier to remember." Tom leaned back in his chair.

Ricky started again. "The *Huks* obtained much-needed arms and ammunition from Philippine army stragglers, from police deserters, and from ambushed enemy patrols in exchange for civilian clothes. They recruited new followers and sought support from the local population as patriots and freedom-fighters."

The conference room door flung open and thudded against the wall. Major General Charles Willoughby filled the open doorframe.

Tom jumped to his feet. "Good morning, sir."

Willoughby stepped through the door and slammed it behind him. "Boys." He nodded at the men.

Boys. Tom's jaw tightened. The image of his six-year-old self bouncing on "Uncle Charles's" lap flashed through his mind. Willoughby was his father's crony, and Tom would never be more than a child to him. At least, not until he could prove himself worthy of being viewed as a man.

Willoughby took off his cap and tossed it on the table, visibly relaxed. "Questions about my report?"

Tom folded the cover on the lengthy manuscript. "Concise and clear, sir."

"Give it back to me in brief then, Tommy." Willoughby crossed his arms.

Tommy. No one had called him that since second grade. *I'm a college graduate,* he wanted to shout. *Worked my way through the FBI's nonsense—on my own, without any help. I deserve a bit of respect, too.* Tom rubbed his throbbing temples. *Get it together. Don't let him see it bothers you.* He forced himself to sit up straighter and locked eyes with Willoughby. "Infiltrate the Huks. Squash the Commies. God bless the Philippines of America."

Willoughby's eyes narrowed, then he threw back his head and let out a raucous laugh. "By God, Tommy, you've got it." He clapped Tom between the shoulder blades hard enough to cause his head to jut. "Next time, remind me to let you edit my reports."

Tom scowled.

A knock sounded at the door. Ricky smoothed back his shiny blond hair, jumped up and strode to the door. "Yes?"

"McCoy," came the voice from the hallway.

Ricky opened the door.

Snake strode in. He glanced over Tom and Ricky, then at Willoughby. His eyes narrowed and his mouth tightened.

"So what did you find?" Tom asked.

Snake removed his eyes from Willoughby with effort, and then turned them on Tom. "I recruited a good snitch for us. Man who worked for me once before. At that time, we gave him the code name *Candy Man*. We called him that because his family owns a sugarcane plantation." He stepped back and gave a smug smile. "He's also a Huk leader."

Tom stiffened.

Before Tom could speak, Willoughby stepped forward, his mouth curled into a sneer. "I know Candy Man. He will be helpful." He walked back to Tom's side at the conference table and muttered under his breath, "The man's a sleaze-ball who'll sing like a canary. Keep your thumb on him."

Willoughby leaned across the table, picked up his cap, and tucked it under his arm. "Continue briefing your men, Tommy. General Yamashita surrendered yesterday. He's been arrested for war crimes. I'm heading to his interrogation now."

Tom straightened. "Sir? There any way I can sit in on that interrogation? Might help to hear what Yamashita has to say with respect to the Huks."

Willoughby fixed Tom in a deadpan stare. "It's none of your concern."

Tom cocked his head. Why wouldn't Willoughby want him there? "Sir, will General Lansdale conduct the interview?"

Willoughby's jaw flexed, a harsh movement in the room's flickering light. "Stay out of it." He turned on his heel and stalked out of the room, slamming the door behind him.

Snake scowled at the door. "Good riddance to bad rubbish."

"What?" Tom asked.

"Never mind." Snake shook his head, then looked at Tom. "You say Willoughby is a trusted family friend?"

Tom grunted. "Yeah." He expelled a long breath. "He's my godfather."

Chapter 4

September 9, 1945
Outskirts of Manila, Philippines

THE SLENDER MAN, known in the Philippines only as *Dr. Wang,* paced around the dank basement he liked to think of as his dungeon. He clenched his teeth and resisted the urge to spit on his prisoner, a member of the powerful Japanese crime enterprise called *Yakuza.* Spitting was distasteful, and if anything, Dr. Wang was a discerning man.

He jutted his chin toward one of his hired henchmen, and the guard backhanded the *wakagashira*—a first lieutenant in the Yakuza family hierarchy—so hard that a bloody tooth flew from the man's mouth. "Where—is—the gold!" Dr. Wang shouted.

The Yakuza kept his head down, refusing to look Dr. Wang in the eye.

"Everything my family owned, everything passed down through generations for hundreds of years, everything *we were*—taken! Taken by the Japanese. Taken by Yakuza. You raped my mother, my sister, my family, my entire country. Raped and pillaged." Dr. Wang nodded, and again one of the three henchmen in the room hit the Yakuza, this time with a fist to the man's head.

The prisoner's head rocked backward, but the man looked up at Dr. Wang with dazed eyes. "Spoils of war," he said, a slow trickle of bloody spittle running down his chin.

"It was *not* spoils of war! This was no war. It was an intrusion with the desire to humiliate our society." Dr. Wang paced to the far side of the basement and stopped with his face only inches from the wet concrete wall. He sucked in a slow, deep breath, fighting for composure. He would maintain control. He would not lay a hand on this man. Never would he soil himself with the blood of another, not when he could easily hire men who relished the power of snuffing out the lives of others.

Dr. Wang smoothed the lapels of his gray suit, straightened his shoulders and purposefully walked back to his prisoner. "What is your connection with Yoshio Kodama?" he asked.

The man looked at him and sneered.

Dr. Wang nodded, and one of the henchmen, a member of the Chinese agency, kicked the Yakuza in the ribs, toppling the chair to which he was tied. The Yakuza prisoner gasped for breath.

"What is your connection to Ryoichi Sasakawa?" Dr. Wang linked his hands behind his back and bent over the prisoner. Ryoichi and Yoshio were admirals in the Japanese Navy involved in a conspiracy to take Chinese gold to Japan. They had been tried and found guilty of war crimes, yet MacArthur, the American general, had pardoned them. "These two know where the stolen NanJing gold is hidden, yes?"

The prisoner mumbled, but Wang couldn't make out the words. He flicked his hand, and two of his henchmen uprighted the man on his chair.

"It's only gold," said the prisoner.

A henchman slapped his face hard enough to cause an echo in the dank basement.

"Only gold," Dr. Wang hissed. "Yes. Yes, it is only gold. Gold will never replace the lives of my family. Yes, for certain there was gold. *My gold.* And other family heirlooms, too. Jewelry and artwork that had been in my family for more than a century, and it still belongs to my family—to me. It is my birthright. And you *will* help me find it."

A guttural laugh escaped the prisoner's mouth. Through tiny slits of swollen eyelids, the man's eyes sparkled crazily. "Come closer, Dr. Wang. I will tell you a secret."

Dr. Wang's chest constricted. Now he would know. He'd broken the man, and now he'd learn the location of his family's wealth, of *his* wealth. He stepped behind the man, lowered his head beside the Yakuza, and bent to put his ear closer to his mouth.

"You will never, ever, find the gold," the prisoner whispered. He tried to spit in Dr. Wang's face, but the spittle hit his chest and dripped down his clothes and onto his shoes. The Yakuza then leaned back his head and roared with laughter.

Dr. Wang rose slowly, pulled a handkerchief from his pocket and wiped his shoes and fine suit coat. He neatly folded it and wiped again. His taciturn expression never changed.

Keeping his eyes locked on the battered face of his prisoner, Dr. Wang reached inside his suit jacket and withdrew a chopstick. He held it parallel to the floor with both hands, then lowered it front of his prisoner's face. Slowly he twisted the chopstick so the prisoner could read the word burned into its side. *NanJing.*

The man looked up at Dr. Wang, the puzzled look in his eyes turning into one of horror. Behind him, one of the henchmen grabbed a fistful of his hair, yanked back his head and slashed his throat. Dr. Wang waited for the man to clean and re-sheathe his weapon, then he handed him the chopstick.

The henchman squeezed the Yakuza's jaw with his large hand, making the gurgling man's mouth open wide. He placed the chopstick between the prisoner's teeth, then closed the dying man's mouth.

Dr. Wang's lips parted in a manner that, on him, might be called a smile. He looked at the Yakuza. He turned to his men. "You know what to do with this piece of rubbish." He turned sharply on his heel and headed up the stairs for afternoon tea.

Chapter 5

September 30, 1945
Manila, Philippines

TOM SAT ON the edge of his bed with his head in his hands. Third migraine this month. He again reminded himself he needed to get a grip on his stopping point with alcohol. It was Snake's moonshine, he was certain. Snake had taken him and Ricky on what he called a "joyride" last evening, showing them his driving skills in what Tom now knew to be a super-charged racing machine. Snake had had the Chevy Special Deluxe brought over from America—North Carolina, to be specific—along with an undocumented amount of moonshine. How in the world the FBI had gone along with that was anyone's guess.

Tom rubbed his neck and stood, grimacing as the minute change in altitude caused his head to swim. He shuffled to the sink, filled a pitcher with water and poured it into his electric percolator. Thank God, the FBI had supplied them with good old American "joe," so he didn't have to drink the bitter coffee loved by Filipinos. He filled a glass with water, shook two Anacin tablets from the metal tin into his hand and threw them back with a gulp. For good measure, he downed two more.

Just as he pulled on his trousers, a knock came at the door. Now by habit, he grabbed his pistol and peered out the peephole. Willoughby.

Tom shoved his gun into the back waistband of his pants and opened the door. He let Willoughby in, then waved away Ricky and Snake as each opened his own door and peered into the hallway to check on Tom.

"What brings you by this morning, sir?" Tom asked.

Willoughby headed toward the percolator, poured a cup of coffee, and downed half of it, black. "Wanted to say goodbye."

Tom squinted. "Goodbye? Which one of us is leaving?"

"That would be me, son. Unless you want to tag along. Might be good for you."

"Oh. Heading back to the States for a reprieve? Tell my folks *hello* from me. I'm not ready to go back home, just yet."

The general shook his head. "Not going to America. I'm going to Japan—with MacArthur."

"With MacAr—to Japan?"

"That's right. I think you should come with us. Your language skills—you'd be a big help to us."

Tom shut his eyes for a moment, willing his head to stop hurting. He opened his eyes and waited for Willoughby to meet his stare. "J. Edgar Hoover gave me this assignment, and I intend to carry it out."

"Hoover, Smoover. I can get your assignment changed."

"I'd rather not, sir, if it pleases you. We've just broken through with Candy Man—got him trusting us, I mean—and now I'm getting leads I'd like to see through to the end."

"He'll be here when you get back."

Tom pressed his lips together. He thought of Judy, and how only three days ago she'd spent her first night in his arms. He didn't want it to be the last. He looked up. "I learned something interesting—something I've wanted to tell you, but I'd hoped to have more concrete information first."

Willoughby raised his cup to his lips, but lowered it without drinking. "What?"

"Seems there's a missing printing press, one the US Mint sent to print money. The plates have been confiscated, perhaps by the Huks, though I don't have confirmation of that yet. And something about war gold. You know, gold that supposedly the Japanese stole from the Chinese and others. Candy Man has a contact who thinks he knows where some of it is hidden."

Willoughby turned away from Tom, walked over to a window, and looked out on the street below. He stood there so long Tom thought the man had forgotten he was there. Tom cleared his throat, and the general turned.

"Stay if you want, but keep your nose out of that printing press business. And don't even think about wasting time looking for lost gold. If the Japs had really buried treasure here, don't you think we'd have found it by now?" Willoughby's face grew red. "Hell, the Philippines would be the richest country on the planet, if that gold had been stashed here. It sank, dammit. Sank on a ship. Everyone knows that."

Tom held up his hands in surrender.

Willoughby turned back to the window, and his voice grew deep and lethal. "And you mind your own damn business, boy. You weren't sent over here to stir up trouble."

"Yes, sir." Tom spoke softly. He'd known Willoughby since he'd been old enough to walk, and never had the man spoken to him with such vehemence.

The Major General's shoulders appeared to sag, then he straightened and turned back to face Tom, his face now frighteningly pleasant. "You're right to want to stay, of course. You've got a job to do—flesh out the Communist Huks. I should've known that once you locked onto your mission, you'd be like a bulldog."

Willoughby's smile appeared artificial, even chilling. Tom stiffened to keep from shuddering.

"MacArthur and I will fly out in the morning." He walked back to the coffee pot, sat down his cup so hard that the china's crash against the countertop echoed in the small kitchenette. He walked toward the door, opened it and turned back to Tom. "They're having a surprise party for me tonight," he said.

"A *surprise*, sir?"

Willoughby's normally stern countenance relaxed, and for a moment, Tom was transported back to the lap of the man he'd known as his godfather, the man who always had a cinnamon candy in his pocket, the man who brought him gifts from exotic places. "I wouldn't be a very good intelligence man if my cohorts were able to keep such an affair a secret, now would I?"

"Uh, no, sir. I suppose not."

"And it seems to be quite the affair. Black tie, of course." He chuckled. "Why don't you bring that little Navy nurse I've seen hanging on your arm, and stop by the officers' club?"

"Well, sir, I don't know—"

"Of course you'll be there!" Willoughby took a step toward the door, then lowered his voice. "Good luck with the Huks. Stay focused."

"Yes, sir. Will do, sir."

"And, kid, keep your nose where it belongs."

Chapter 6

September 30, 1945
The Officers Club
Manila, Philippines

CIGAR SMOKE CURLED upward from each table, swirled around sparkling chandeliers and gathered in a blue-gray haze under the ceiling. If Judy were still on the family farm in Oklahoma, she'd be wary of cloud cover like that. Especially the way some of the smoke spiraled, creating tiny funnel clouds.

Tom coughed and fanned the smoke away from Judy.

"It's all right, Tom. Really."

"They need an exhaust fan in here." Tom continued to flap his arms. "This is ridiculous."

"Now, now, now," Judy scolded.

"You can't even see through the smoke in this place."

"Settle down." She stirred the tall glass of punch—at least, what once had been punch. Now it was a bit of vodka and white rum over chunks of pineapple and mango. She stabbed a piece of pineapple with her straw, brought it to her lips, and sucked out the liquor.

Tom watched her, grinning, his bright blue eyes twinkling in the candlelight.

An involuntary shiver played on her spine. In high school, she'd been too tall, too gangly, too *country*. She dated the band's lead trumpet player throughout her senior year, and before that, she casually dated a boy from the next farm over. And now, here she sat across the table from the star quarterback. Her eyes scanned his dark hair, stylishly combed back. Compared to the military cuts, it was long—long enough to show off his natural wave. But below that hair was his jaw line. The sexiest jaw line she'd ever seen. A mixture of sensitivity and strength, it reminded her of a Hollywood movie star.

"Want another drink?"

Knowing he watched, she teased the pineapple with her tongue.

"Or maybe we should just call it a night. What do you think?"

Judy giggled. "No, silly. We just got here. And I've never before, in my entire life, seen so much brass in one room."

"Brass? Is that what it is? I thought it was smoke."

She laughed. "Okay, Funny Man. Yes, I'd like another drink. Another of those potent punches."

Tom took her glass, allowing his fingers to linger over hers, sending more delightful ripples of electricity over her spine. With his intense blue eyes never leaving hers, he lifted her glass in the air.

Instantaneously, a waiter grabbed the glass. Another server slid a fresh glass of punch onto the table. Fruit garnish dangled off the rim. "Here you go, my darling," Tom said, scooting the glass toward her, his eyes still holding hers. "Now, a penny for your thoughts."

"No way. My thoughts are much more valuable than that." She took a long sip of the cool beverage. Besides, there's no way she'd ever tell him how far out of her league he was. If he knew she was just an awkward country girl, he'd be taking up with one of the exotically beautiful Filipina women that filled this island. Panic stabbed through her. What would happen when she took him to the farm to meet her parents? Her mother, with her strong arms and clear skin that had never once known a hint of makeup? Her father, a burly man with a terse vocabulary and a quick temper? And . . . .

Ronnie. Ronnie was no longer there. He'd died on the USS *Arizona* a week before his nineteenth birthday.

"Okay, a quarter. Surely your thoughts are worth a quarter."

"There you are!" Major General Charles Willoughby pulled a chair to their table and sat, a fat cigar propped between his fingers.

Judy jumped to her feet, almost spilling her drink. She squared her shoulders and saluted.

Major General Willoughby laughed. "At ease, my dear. I just came over her to visit with my godson."

"G-godson?" Judy dropped back into her seat, bumping the table. This time, her drink tipped precariously.

Tom grabbed it and steadied it.

Had she heard correctly? *Godson?* She knew Tom came from a pedigreed Bostonian family, but he was the godson of Major General Charles Willoughby?

"Sure wish you'd change your mind and come to Japan with me," Willoughby said.

Tom shook his head. "I think I need to stay here for a while."

Willoughby cast a quick glance at Judy. "Yes. Yes, I think I'm starting to understand. Huks, ducks. It's a WAVE that has you staying put."

Heat sprouted behind Judy's cheeks and burned across her face.

"Oh, I'm sorry!" Tom said. "Where are my manners? Uncle Charles, this is my, uh, my girlfriend. Judith Ray. Judy, Major General Charles Willoughby."

Judy again clamored to her feet, but Willoughby beat her to it. He moved the bulky cigar to his left hand and extended his right. "My pleasure, ma'am."

Judy reached to shake his hand, but instead, he grabbed her from behind the neck and kissed her sloppily on the lips. Before she could protest, he released her.

Resisting the urge to wipe her mouth, she forced a smile and sat. Polite or not, appropriate or not, she grabbed her drink with both hands and drank greedily. Uncle Charles had left a bad taste on her lips.

Willoughby grabbed a martini off a passing tray and dropped into his seat. "Did I tell you I spoke to your father last week?"

Tom's clear blue eyes clouded. "No."

"He still thinks you're sowing wild oats." Willoughby laughed raucously.

Tom turned away from him. "Yeah, I bet he does," he said dryly.

Willoughby slapped Tom's shoulder. "He means well, son. He means well. He just wants you to come home and settle down."

"Well, I'm settled down, and this is my home. For now."

"I told him you were doing an important service for our country, but he didn't want to hear about it."

"Figures."

Willoughby laughed again, spilling cigar ashes over the table. He was not an especially large man, yet he seemed to take up a great deal of space.

Judy scooted her chair closer to Tom. It didn't appear that Willoughby was in a hurry to leave, so she concentrated on her drink and on the handsome man next to her. Although she couldn't help but think of the future—of the day when they were married and had several little ones running around the farm—for now, she was content. Tom had introduced her as his *girlfriend*. She continued to slurp the potent punch. His *girlfriend*. Heat bourgeoned from deep within her, burned through her veins and warmed her skin. This man, this unbelievably intelligent FBI agent, this handsome college quarterback, this sexy man with the sensitive jaw line and movie-star good looks—he was her *boyfriend*.

And on this day, nothing else really mattered.

Chapter 7

February 14, 1946
Manila, Philippines

TOM LOOKED AROUND the candlelit dining room of Manila's Hilton Hotel, seeking refuge from Judith Ray's question. No one came to his rescue. Her delicate fingers touched the back of his hand, and he fought to keep from pulling away as if she'd bitten him.

"Tom?" she said. "Surely you must have had these same questions yourself, yes? Don't you wonder where our relationship is heading?"

Tom looked back at her, his smile stretched too tightly across his teeth. "I'm having fun, Judy, aren't you?"

Judy blinked hard. "Why . . . yes. But . . ." Her voice cracked, and she folded her hands in her lap and stared down at them.

A waiter appeared at Tom's side with a water pitcher. "Refill, sir?" Without waiting for an answer, the man filled Tom's glass, then Judy's.

After the man finished and walked away, Tom cleared his throat. "Look, Judy, I really like you. I think—"

"Like me? You *like* me!" Judy's voice grew shrill. "What am I, a puppy?"

Tom glanced around him, embarrassed by the curious faces turning their way. "Shhh. What I mean is—Judy, I care about you. I care about you an awful lot."

Judy wadded her napkin from her lap and threw it on the table, her face red.

Quickly Tom reached across the table and grabbed her hand as she scooted back her chair. Obviously, he'd given her the wrong answer. He lowered his head—and his voice. "Judy, I—I *love* you."

"Oh, Tom!" Judy's eyes glistened and she stood, leaning across the table to grab Tom's face in her hands. She kissed him so hard their teeth collided against his lower lip.

A smattering of applause broke out from nearby tables, and Judy drew back, dabbing at her eyes as she beamed a smile at her sudden fans.

Tom felt hot. And sick. He forced a smile, ran a tongue across the inside of his lower lip, tasted blood. *Dear God!* These people though he'd proposed to her!

Across the table, Judy settled into her chair, talking so fast Tom couldn't focus on her words. He forced himself to zero in on her lips, concentrate on what she was saying.

"—guess I'm just a white picket fence kind of girl. Or, oh, I don't know, maybe a southern mansion kind of girl would be accurate, too, though I'm not above living a modest lifestyle, Thomas. I've always had that *Gone With the Wind* dream, I suppose, but haven't we all? I mean, every young girl dreams of her Ashley Wilkes—I'm no Rhett-Butler-chaser, mind you—but I am quite sure I could be the Melody to a man like Ashley."

Thomas? Since when does she call me Thomas? Tom reached for his water glass and downed about two-thirds of it just as the waiter again appeared at his table with a cloth-wrapped bottle of champagne.

"Compliments of the house," the waiter said, smiling broadly. "And congratulations, sir, madam." He nodded to each of the two in turn, then ceremoniously uncorked the champagne bottle to Judy's applause. He first filled Judy's glass, then Tom's.

Judy lifted her glass in the air. "To us!"

Tom had never been to war, but he suddenly recognized the feeling of shell shock. He hadn't proposed, had he? He hadn't even asked this woman to go steady. Tom stared at the champagne, envious of the bubbles that managed to float to the top of his glass and escape. He tried in his mind to rewind the last several minutes of their conversation. He'd told her he liked her. She'd gotten angry. He'd pacified her by telling her he—oh, no! He'd used the L-word.

"Honey?"

He met Judy's eyes, which were suddenly filled with concern. He lifted his glass, and her eyes brightened as if he'd flipped a switch. Could it really be this easy to please her? Or this hard to back out of a situation he hadn't meant to create?

Their crystal champagne flutes chimed pleasantly as they toasted, and Tom gulped his entire glass in one long swallow. Before he could stop himself, he refilled the flute and guzzled it down, as well. He'd started filling it a third time, when he realized Judy was staring at him.

"Pardon me," he said, then topped off her glass before finishing filling his own. "This is quite refreshing, isn't it?"

Judy nodded, and Tom lifted his flute in another toast. "Happy Valentine's Day, Judy."

She smiled, and touched her glass to his. "Happy Valentine's Day, Tom. May this be the first of many we'll share together."

Chapter 8

February 23, 1946
Manila, Philippines

TOM CURLED HIS arm around Judy's waist in a protective measure as he ushered her through the throng of restless onlookers. Snake kept glancing back at him, and in turn, Tom often looked back at Ricky, who'd nod that all was okay. The quartet was on edge, though so far the crowd seemed more curious than agitated.

Sick heaviness had settled in Tom's stomach. No matter popular opinion, he still believed General Tomoyuki Yamashita was being railroaded.

Raising a hand to deflect a cardboard placard with the mistranslated English words *Hung Him!,* Tom followed Snake's lead. Judy wanted a front-row vantage point to Yamashita's public execution, but Tom insisted they avoid the chance of appearing in any of the photographs the press would be snapping.

Snake's broad shoulders cleared an area where the four could stand together off to one side, still in clear view of the gallows.

Judy pointed toward an area directly in front of the scaffold where Filipino soldiers monitored the crowd. "Can't we go over there?"

Tom shook his head. "We can see fine from here." He looked over her head and caught Ricky's eyes, then cocked his head toward a side door of the building in front of which the gallows stood. Ricky gave an almost imperceptible nod, then trained his eyes on the door.

Tom guessed General Yamashita was being interrogated behind that door. His jaw twitched. He'd give anything to be privy to that conversation, to see if Edward Lansdale treated Yamashita with the dignity a general deserved, or if instead he belittled and berated the man.

"—listening to me? Honestly, Thomas, your mind is a million miles away." Judy pawed Tom's arm playfully, but her pout betrayed her petulance.

"Sorry, darling." Tom took a deep breath. "Guess I just never expected to watch a man hang. Especially a man who is being used as a sacrificial lamb."

Judy unlinked her arm from Tom's. "Sacrificial lamb? How can you say such a thing?"

"I can't imagine he's getting a fair shake in there, can you? I mean, if nothing else, it seems he'd be worth more to the US and to the Philippines alive, than dead, doesn't it?" Tom grimaced. "Especially if they believe he knows where the stolen war gold is hidden."

Judy's painted lips compressed into a thin red stripe. "If there ever was stolen war gold, you mean."

Snake turned to face the two. "Well, if no war loot was stolen, what purpose would they have for hanging him?"

Judy's face flushed and her eyes flashed. "What purpose? *What purpose?* Tell me you didn't just say that!" She turned to Tom. "Surely you don't feel that way, Tom."

"No. No, I don't. I don't doubt for a minute that the Japanese committed atrocious, unnecessary crimes of war in China. Nor do I doubt that spoils of war were captured and brought to the Philippines. In fact, that's why I don't understand this hanging."

Tom felt a finger poke against his back and turned to see Ricky cock his head toward the side door of the building. He followed Ricky's gaze.

The door opened a scant few inches, a pale hand gripping the inside doorknob. Tom narrowed his gaze onto that slice of darkness, peering intently, hoping to see a face. The door closed, and Tom huffed.

"I don't think you have a clear understanding of what General Yamashita required his men to do," Judy said. "He was the person who gave the order to his troops. He was the one who commanded them to rape women and even children, to rob families, to burn down homes, to pillage entire villages and leave nothing behind but scars." Splotches of color appeared on Judy's chest and neck.

Tom drew in a long, slow breath. He should have kept his mouth shut.

Within a few seconds, the door opened again, just a few inches. Again, a hand gripped the knob. Whoever stood there was waiting to open the door. But waiting for what? It wasn't as if the press of onlookers would disappear. These people—vultures, in Tom's eyes—were here to see an execution, and they wouldn't leave without a carcass.

A barrage of shouts and cheers caused Tom to protectively hug Judith Ray against him. She pushed her palms against his ribs, loosening his hold.

"Let me go! I want to see! Those Japanese bastards killed my brother at Pearl Harbor!" She looked up at him fiercely.

General Yamashita, flanked by Philippine soldiers, exited the double doors of the building. More members of the Philippine Army followed and culled around the general, ushering him toward the gallows pole.

The general didn't flinch. He held up his head, and even from where Tom stood, it was easy to see he'd been battered.

"The Tiger of Malaya doesn't look so dangerous now," Snake said solemnly.

Tom looked at General Yamashita, his bruised, oval face and balding head appearing anything but dangerous. He was a man, nothing more than a man, who was taking the hit for the emperor.

The side door! Tom craned his head to look around a man with a camera who'd stepped in front of him. The door was again closing, this time of its own accord. Off to one side of the door, Colonel Edward Lansdale looked over his shoulder as he walked away, nodding toward another man. Tom followed Lansdale's glance. A big, tall man wearing a white *barong tagalong* walked in the opposite direction, head bent down. Tom had seen the figure before, but couldn't place a face. Then the man glanced back at Lansdale, and Tom's mouth dropped open. It was the priest from outside his window, this time no cassock. *Why was he there?*

Tom watched as the two men hustled away from the side door, away from one other, each quickly blending into the crowd of onlookers. Lansdale panned the crowd, as if searching for a face. Tom quickly stepped backward, ducking behind the man with the camera.

"What on earth are you doing, Tom?" Judy frowned and turned back to watch as the soldiers held General Yamashita's arms, leading him up the steps to the gibbet.

Tom straightened. He had no reason to worry about Lansdale seeing him, after all. Practically everyone in Manila and her surrounding boroughs had turned out to see the hanging. Certainly, the priest would not have been there to give Yamashita last rites. No, he wasn't there for any logical reason. Tom pursed his lips. The man would have worn a cassock, and he likely would have walked out among the soldiers. He was there for Lansdale, not for Yamashita. And not to offer last rites, either.

A shrill cheer brought Tom back to the present. Judy jumped up and down on the balls of her feet, joining in the horrific merriment of the historic moment. Tom again pulled her close, and she looked into his face, her own growing more solemn.

Tom focused on the scene before him, his stomach knotting as a small, stout Philippine man with caramel skin and a wide nose stood to one side of General Yamashita, proudly holding the noose. The look in the man's dark eyes alarmed Tom, even when seen from a distance. He looked like evil incarnate.

A Philippine general stepped forward and addressed General Yamashita. "For the crimes committed by the men under your command, including the massacre of over one hundred thousand Filipino civilians here in Manila, you, General Tomoyuki Yamashita, will be hanged until you are dead."

The crowd roared approval so loudly that Tom flinched. The dark-skinned soldier with the vile eyes raised his hand, and the throng silenced.

The Philippine general jutted his chin. "Do you have any last words?"

General Yamashita looked boldly over the crowd through swollen eyelids. "I believe I have done my duty to the best of my ability throughout the whole war. Now at the time of my death and before God I have nothing to be ashamed of. Please remember me to the American officers who defended me."

The malevolent-looking soldier roughly yanked the noose over Yamashita's head and tied a black scarf around the man's eyes. He formally stepped backward, clicking his heels together and arrogantly squaring his shoulders.

Tom put his hand on Judy's face, gently guiding her into his chest so that she wouldn't have to see the horror of a man hanged. Before he could nestle his nose in her hair, she yanked away from him.

"Stop it, Tom," she whispered, her voice fierce. "I want to see this." She turned and lifted her satisfied countenance toward the scaffolding, watching the last seconds of Yamashita's life.

Tom's mouth went dry.

The Philippine general raised his arm into the air. The murmuring crowd hushed. When all was perfectly silent, the man lowered his arm and the door beneath Yamashita's feet opened, dropping his body and audibly snapping his neck.

Tom turned away.

Judy clapped, joining the tens of thousands of others who gleefully watched this man die.

When he turned back, Snake and Ricky were watching Yamashita's body sway, stunned looks on their faces. Flash bulbs popped as photographers snapped photo after gruesome photo. Tom looked at Judy, confused by the look in her eyes. It was one of . . . of fulfillment . . . of *peace*. This hadn't bothered her at all.

"You don't get it, do you, Tom?" She looked at him, a mixture of disappointment and sadness briefly clouding her clear gaze.

Tom lifted his hands, and unsure of what to do with them, he placed them on Judy's shoulders. "I just—I've never seen a man hanged before."

Judy shrugged. "Me either." She looked again at Yamashita, then back at Tom. "But that bastard deserved it. I'm glad I was here. I want to see every drop of blood in his body turn cold."

Tom's lips parted, but he didn't know what to say. This woman was either crazy, or gutsy, or both.

"Look, Tom, I'm not heartless." She jabbed a finger toward Yamashita's now-motionless body. "That man—that *beast* of a man—he was the cause of my brother's death. He ordered the slaughter not only of many Japanese and Filipino soldiers and civilians, but of many American soldiers, too." The color of her face deepened, and her eyes grew dark with rage. "And then he stood there—" She pointed again. "He *stood there* and had the nerve to thank some American officers for defending him. Well, I don't believe it! I don't believe any American officer would defend that man after he gave orders for so many of our own soldiers to die. After he gave orders that caused my brother to—" Judy's voice caught in her throat and tears sprang to her eyes.

Tom again tried to pull her to him, and this time she allowed it, burrowing her face in his chest, letting go of God only knows how many years of pent-up anger and grief.

Chapter 9

February 23, 1946
Honk Kong, China

DR. WANG STARED at the creased, yellowed photograph of his family, long since murdered. Decades ago as a teenager in China, he'd folded it into a small square and carried it in a hole he'd torn into the waistband of his underwear when he'd run from the Japanese soldiers who'd massacred his family. He now held the photograph close to his eyes, peering intently at his mother's hand.

His family's wealth was impressive, even by the high standards of China's elite. He remembered the now-priceless paintings that graced the walls of their palace-like mansion, the imperial cloisonné enamel crane censers from the 1700s, the matching rare *Famille Rose* vases adorning his mother's dressing table, the white jade teacup from which she sipped tea each morning while she powdered her face. But it was her hand in the photo he studied now. Specifically, the heirloom ring on her right hand.

He reached into a desk drawer and pulled out a magnifying glass and held it over the photograph. The emerald in the bridal ring was enormous—larger than the pupil in his mother's eye, he remembered his father saying—surrounded by diamond-encrusted gold curls. The ring was attached to an emerald wrist bracelet by a thin strand of diamonds set in gold. Minus the bracelet, it was identical to the ring on the Japanese geisha's hand. The geisha he'd seen in the magazine at the bathhouse. The same geisha his men were delivering to him at any moment.

Sweat prickled his underarms at the thought of the geisha. She was his private reward, his personal celebration of Yamashita's hanging today in the Philippines. He wanted to be there—*should* have been there—to watch the man die, but when he'd seen the photo of this woman wearing his mother's ring, his priorities became clear.

Dr. Wang kissed the photo, wrapped it in rice paper, and tucked it into the leather-bound, gilt-edged booklet where he recorded all things secret and precious to him. He slid the booklet into an intricately carved ivory box, locked the box and returned it to his desk drawer, which he also locked. He slid the key into his pocket, then lifted the tiny goblet into the air, turned to the mirror and toasted himself. "One more success."

The warm lychee vodka slid easily across his tongue and down his throat, and since he was alone, he smacked his lips and smiled at his reflection. The tinkling chime of the front door alerted him that his prize had arrived. He felt a familiar stiffness return to his groin, but mentally forced it to subside. He crossed the room to his bookshelf, opened another box, pulled out a smooth, polished chopstick, and turned it in his thin fingers until he read the word burned there: *NanJing.* Dr. Wang slid the chopstick into his suit jacket, then straightened the collar and smoothed the lapels. He again apprised himself in the mirror. He looked handsome in gray.

Dr. Wang walked toward the receiving parlor, his pulse thrumming evenly in his ears. Though he'd seen the geisha's photo, studied it even, he was unprepared for her beauty in the flesh. The woman's heart-shaped face was lightly rice-powdered in white, not heavily made up like the cosmetic masks some geishas wore. She appeared ethereal, and the natural health of her skin shone through. Dr. Wang let his gaze rove her satin clad body. Tiny, pale feet peeped below her kimono, and bare ivory hands reached toward the serving tray his butler held.

She did not wear the ring.

Dr. Wang's blood pressure rose. He finally raised his eyes to look again at her face.

Confusion flickered over the young woman's smooth features. Her eyebrows twitched slightly.

Dr. Wang smiled. Of course she would be confused. She never would've expected a Chinese man to request a geisha.

The woman quickly regained her professional composure and struck a coy pose. She elegantly lifted the crystal glass of lychee vodka, holding it both hands as she crossed the floor to offer it to Dr. Wang. His eyes found her wasp-like waist, tied with a fuchsia sash, then traveled upward to her flawless neck and throat, where he watched her pulse flutter beneath the skin.

"For you," she said, bowing before him as she offered the small glass.

He took the glass and swallowed the vodka. This time, it did not taste as sweet. He flung the glass against the wall where it shattered into sparkling shards that covered the floor.

The geisha drew back and buried her face in her arm.

Dr. Wang grabbed the perfectly wrapped coif of hair atop her head and pulled the waif of a woman to her feet. "Where is the ring?"

Her dark, almond-shaped eyes grew wide and she trembled.

Dr. Wang lifted a hand, moving his finger almost imperceptibly. The two men who'd brought the geisha to him each grabbed one of her arms. The woman struggled, her eyes darting to the men who'd moments ago treated her like a queen.

"Where is the ring?" Dr. Wang demanded, his voice full of poison.

The geisha shook her head. "What? I don't know—"

The henchman on her left backhanded her face, smearing the perfect red O of her lipsticked mouth. She let out a cry.

Dr. Wang snapped his fingers, and his butler produced the magazine, opened to the photo of the geisha provocatively peering out from behind a fan. Dr. Wang held the magazine before the woman's face as his henchman gripped a fistful of her hair, forcing her to look at the page.

"The ring you wore in this picture. Where is it?"

She tried to shake her head, but the man yanked her hair, holding her face still.

"I d-do not—I do not know. It was a—a prop. My costume. It is not mine."

Dr. Wang flung the magazine to the side and leaned close to her face. "Where did it come from? Who gave it to you to wear?"

Tears drew lines down her powdered face, creating roads that traveled down her neck and into her cleavage. She trembled and her swelling lip quivered as she spoke. "I do not know. It was there. Lying there. On top of my kimono. Part of my costume. I don't know who put it there."

Dr. Wang nodded toward his men, and they dragged the woman toward a chair the butler brought. The men shoved her onto the chair, and one untied her sash while the other held her arms behind the chair. Her kimono fell open, revealing her pale, quivering body. The woman bent forward in an effort to cover her nakedness, and one of the henchmen again grabbed her hair, yanking her upright. "Sit still," he hissed.

Dr. Wang walked calmly across the floor until he stood in front of the quaking woman. "Who has the ring?"

The woman shook her head in tiny, jerking movements. "I do not know."

Dr. Wang held his finger close to the woman's cheek, but did not touch her. He allowed his finger to trace the outline of her chin, her throat and down the curve of her bare breast. "Swine," he said. "Japanese swine."

Delicately, almost reverently, he leaned forward, reached into her hair, and pulled out one of the enameled skewers that held her now-lopsided coif in place. He flung the skewer across the room, causing her to flinch. Dr. Wang stood and looked at the woman again, tilting his head to one side. He reached into his jacket and pulled out the chopstick, holding it before the woman's eyes for her to read. She panted short, shallow breaths.

Dr. Wang lifted the chopstick into the air, thrilled to see horror in the woman's eyes. He slowly moved his hand behind her head, sliding the chopstick into her hair in place of the skewer he'd removed. He held out his hand, and his butler placed a coil of rope into his palm. Dr. Wang held up the rope for the woman to see. "As your General Yamashita, so you." He reached out his hand, offering the rope to his henchman, who nodded, his mouth twisting into a vicious smile.

Dr. Wang dusted the hemp from his hands, reached for a fresh goblet of warm vodka and lifted it into the air. "One more success."

Chapter 10

July 12, 1946
Manila, Philippines

THE HEAVY CIGARETTE smoke hanging in the air swirled into white curls. Tom waved it away.

Candy Man either didn't seem to notice or didn't care, and he took another long drag off his cigarette and blew smoke toward the ceiling. "I don't care what they say. There's gold. There is definitely gold. I've seen it with my own eyes. I know where some of it is buried."

Ricky looked at Snake, then at Tom, and one eyebrow lifted.

"Oh, I believe you," Tom said. "At least, I *want* to believe you." He shrugged. "I trust no man like I trust my own eyes." He smiled and sipped from the dirty glass, hoping the alcohol would kill whatever the crust was that lurked on the lip of the glass of rotgut whiskey.

Voices rose in the front of the dingy bar. Tom looked toward the commotion. A man pressed a gun barrel to the head of the man sitting across from him. Tom held his breath. A few other patrons looked on, but no one seemed surprised or even upset, and after a moment, the man with the gun holstered his weapon and picked up his hand of cards. *Huks.* Tom and his crew had made several visits to the bar that seemed to be a regular Huk hangout, and each time, he'd seen fights break out. So far, no one had been shot, but he figured, given time, it was inevitable.

"You saying you don't trust me?" Candy Man narrowed his eyes at Tom.

Tom held out his palm. "The proof is in the pudding. I'm only saying that seeing is believing."

Candy Man nodded vigorously. "That is what I mean. I have seen, so I believe."

Ever the peacemaker, Snake held up his whiskey glass. "To believing!"

Ricky and Tom lifted their glasses in toast, and Candy Man, wearing a confused smile, clinked his glass with theirs. "To believing!"

The raucous noise in the bar quieted a few decibels, and the quartet turned to see why. Two well-dressed Filipinos walked in.

Candy Man and Snake exchanged a quick glance, then both dodged behind a three-panel rice-paper screen.

Tom leaned toward Snake. "Who's that?"

"That's Luis Taruc." Tom tried to imprint the face into his memory. "Know the name, but have never seen him."

Candy Man sat up and arched his neck like a proud rooster, clearly pleased to have important information to share. "Luis Taruc is the head Huk."

Tom glanced from Snake to Candy Man and back. "Head of what?"

Candy Man rolled his eyes. "He is the head *Hukbalahap*. The leader of the Huks, that's who."

Ricky sipped from his glass, looking at Snake.

Candy Man leaned toward Tom. "You didn't know? He was elected to the Philippine House of Representatives."

Tom leaned back in his chair. "If he's so important, then what's he doing in a dive like this?" He ducked his head and covertly watched Taruc. Everyone in the room paid him respect, if only with their eyes and nods. Taruc took a table near the dusty front window—clearly not a man for hiding—and began talking with the Filipino sitting there.

Candy Man dared a glance at Taruc, then dodged back behind the screen. "He wasn't allowed to serve in Congress. They said he fixed the election, and they barred him from the House." He shook his head and huffed. "The election was not fixed. Taruc won fair and square. His people love him. That's why he is here. We are his people. He is our leader."

Tom swirled the whiskey in his glass. "Then why are you hiding?"

Candy Man's eyes grew large. "Being seen with three FBI stiffs ain't good for my career, if you know what I mean."

A smile played at Tom's lips. "So who's the other man with him?"

Candy Man grinned. "Ah, that's Jose Alejandrino."

"He is another Huk official," Snake added. "What's their relationship?"

Candy Man leaned forward and lowered his voice. "They have been meeting about being cheated out of the election, I feel certain, and maybe even how he plans to strike a deal with President Manual Roxas." Candy Man threw back his entire glass of whiskey and let out a satisfied, "Ahhhh."

Ricky eyed the man. "What is your relationship with Taruc?"

Candy Man thrust out his chest. "We are close. I showed him some of the places where the gold is buried." He motioned toward the bar, and a scruffy man wearing an eye-patch carried over a bottle of whiskey and refilled Candy Man's glass.

Tom took a sip from his own glass and grimaced. "If you showed Taruc where the gold is buried, why hasn't he dug it up? Why didn't he buy the election with all that wealth?"

"You don't understand. Knowing where the gold is buried and getting it out of the ground are two different things. Taruc is a Huk, as I am a Huk. If a Huk digs a big hole in the side of the mountain, people will notice. The Philippine Army will notice. They will steal the gold from under us as soon as we find it. They will kill us." He leaned forward and spoke in a low whisper. "Do not doubt what I am saying. There is enough gold buried there to buy the whole Philippine country. One day . . . ." He glanced around, caught the eyes of the bartender, straightened and took a drink of whiskey.

Tom swirled the whiskey in his glass. "I want to see it."

Ricky nodded, his eyes bright. "Yeah."

Candy Man shook his head and pressed his lips together.

"You don't have to show me the gold, then," Tom said. "Just point out where it's buried."

Candy Man looked at his drink, then at each of the men in turn. "Okay. I will take you to where it is buried, but I will not get out of the car. You will not get out of the car. We will drive, and I will point. That is all. We clear?"

Tom grinned, reached across the table and offered his handshake. "Clear."

Candy Man pulled away, scooting back his chair. "Put your hand down! We do not shake hands." His eyes darted around the room to see if anyone had noticed Tom's extended hand. "I will take you, but we do not shake hands. No sign of a deal. Someone could misunderstand. No handshakes."

Tom held up his hands. "Okay, no handshakes."

Snake held up his car keys. "Let's ride."

Candy Man stood, but remained behind the screen. "You go out the front door. I'll go out the back door and meet you at your car." He took another fearful peek at Taruc, then slithered along the wall to the rear exit.

Tom shrugged and tossed down enough bills to cover their drinks and a nice tip. "Let's go see some gold."

⤙▬◉ ◉▬⤚

Tom took a long swig of water from the quart jar, then covertly placed it between his feet, leaned forward from the backseat of Snake's Chevy and passed the quart of moonshine to Candy Man. Though he and the boys had stopped drinking half an hour ago, they wanted their informant drunk. The more Candy Man drank, the more he talked. "Why did Luis Taruc get so angry at his government? Was it for not recognizing the Huks' operations against the Japanese?"

Candy Man took the quart jar, pulled a sip from it and wiped his arm on his sleeve. He held up the jar. "This is good liquor, this moonshine. I like it."

Snake laughed and took the jar from Candy Man, pretended to take a sip, then handed it back to the man, who took another sip. Snake glanced back at Ricky and winked. Candy Man looked at Snake, then at Tom, then directly behind him at Ricky. He pointed to a rutted dirt road off the curving road that led up the mountainside. "Turn here, Snake." Candy Man twisted in his seat to look at Tom.

"Over there." Candy Man pointed to a dry rocky area that sloped down into the gorge. "That is where the Japanese buried the gold."

Snake slowed the car and pulled to the side of the road.

"No." Candy Man gripped Snake's arm. "Do not stop. Keep going. We don't want to be seen here."

Snake glanced back at Tom.

"Who will see us here?" Tom asked.

"The gold is always being watched. Always guarded."

"By whom?"

"Father Jose Antonio Diaz has someone watching it all the time."

Tom slid forward to the edge of the backseat and draped his arms over the seat in front of him. "Father *who?*"

Candy Man crossed himself. "No one. Never mind."

"You said *Father.* Do you mean the priest who wears the big gold cross around his neck?"

Candy Man's mouth fell open. He closed it slowly, then turned toward Snake. "Please. We must leave."

"Relax," Snake drawled. "No one is up here. I watched the road behind us all the way up the mountain. No one followed us, and no one turned onto the road behind us." He peered out the car window. "Look. You'd see a cloud of road dust if someone approached."

Candy Man looked all round him, then sank back into the car seat.

"Let's get out and take a look around." Tom nodded toward the supposed burial site.

Snake opened the car door and stepped out.

"No! We shouldn't be here!" Candy Man grabbed for Tom's hand.

Tom pulled away. "Want us to leave? Really? Come on, don't be a fraidy cat. Like Snake said, there's no one here."

"There is always someone here," Candy Man whispered, his dark eyes large.

Ricky slid across the backseat and climbed out of the car. The three men walked across the dirt road toward the area Candy Man had pointed out to them.

Candy Man opened his car door and stood beside it, but would go no farther. "Please. Come back. It is very dangerous."

Tom looked at Ricky, who shrugged.

"He's really frightened," Ricky said.

Tom grinned. "Hey, Candy Man?"

"Yes? Yes, please come back."

"If you want us to leave, tell me about the man you mentioned a moment ago. The priest."

Candy Man shook his head, looked around and again crossed himself. He motioned for Tom to come closer.

Tom nudged Snake and cocked an eyebrow at Ricky. The three men turned and headed back to Candy Man. "Okay, tell me."

"He is the priest with the gold cross. Yes. Father Diaz." Candy Man glanced all around again, his eyes like baseballs.

"Where is his church?"

Candy Man put his hands together as if in prayer. "Please, please. I have said too much already. He is powerful. Very powerful."

Snake and Ricky both looked at Tom. "The priest is powerful?" Tom prompted. "How is he powerful?"

Candy Man looked over his shoulder, then up at the sky. He lowered his voice to barely a whisper. "They are graves."

"Graves?" Tom said. "What are you talking about?"

"The gold tunnels." Candy Man's slurring whisper sounded like a hiss. "The burial sites are also graves. When the Japanese blasted shut the tunnels where they hid the gold, they buried alive all the soldiers they had made into slaves." He leaned his face close to Tom. "Their spirits still live here, and the priest uses them to guard the gold."

Despite the warm afternoon sun, Snake shuddered. "You don't have to tell me twice. Let's get the hell outta here." He rounded the Chevy and swung open his car door as Candy Man climbed back into the passenger seat. "You boys coming?"

The men reluctantly returned to the car and clamored in. Snake started the car. "Hand me that moonshine."

Tom reached for the jar of water in the back floorboard, but Snake already had his hand on the real thing and gulped down a long swallow. He put the car in drive and swung the behemoth around with precision and speed Tom wouldn't have thought possible. "Let's get off this mountain before it gets dark."

"Good idea," Candy Man said. "We do not want to make the spirits angry. They believe it belongs to them."

"What do you mean?" Tom asked. "What belongs to them?"

"The gold," Candy Man said, his slurring voice somehow reverent. "Now you know why Taruc hasn't touched the gold. He is afraid. It is no longer Japanese gold or even Chinese gold. It is the gold of the spirits."

Chapter II

May 11, 1947
Manila, Philippines

TOM RAN HIS fingertips down the length of Judy's arm as she lay curled against him on the green sofa. He bowed his head and kissed her pale shoulder.

"You're going to miss me more than you think you will, Thomas Warren." Judy looked up at him, her eyes shining and bright.

"Yes, I will."

She turned and nestled against his chest, and Tom fingered her soft hair. Whether he wanted to say it aloud, or not, he'd fallen hard for this woman. He sometimes told her he loved her now, and it was true. Marriage was the last thing he wanted, though, and it was something Judy brought up more and more often as her tour of duty neared its end.

"You could come with me, you know." Judy raised her head and met his eyes. "Back to the States. We could . . . I don't know. Get married?"

Tom felt breath rush from his lungs before he realized he'd sighed.

Tears sprang to Judy's eyes.

"Oh, honey, don't." He kissed the top of her head and she buried her face against him. "You know I love you, Judy. I can't . . . I can't leave the Philippines right now. I still have a job to do."

She rose on one elbow, then pushed herself upright, her face red. "You could leave if you wanted to. You've been here a year and a half. Surely they'd understand if you wanted to return home and settle down."

Settle down. The words sank into Tom's brain. "I can't leave. My work here isn't finished. I've made a commitment, and I don't back away from commitments."

"What about your commitment to me?" Judy's lower lip protruded in the sexy way that made Tom want to kiss her.

Mesmerized, he leaned forward, but she pushed him back.

"Please? Please, Tom."

Tom shook his head. "No. No. No way I'm leaving when I'm this close." He held his index finger and thumb closely together.

Judy stood quickly and walked toward the bedroom. "Then I'm staying, too."

Tom crossed the room, reaching for her. He took her by the shoulders. "No, sweetheart." An apologetic smile played at his lips and he pulled Judy into a hug, rubbing her back.

Judy drew a finger along Tom's jawline. She leaned into Tom and kissed him, delicately at first, then deeper.

Tom ran his hands along her spine, down to her small waist and to the curve of her hips. He pulled her against him, and as heat ignited between them, he slid an arm to her knees and lifted her off the floor, carrying her to his bed.

Tonight, her last night in the Philippines, would be one he'd make sure she'd remember.

Chapter 12

TOM NODDED TO Snake. The man gave him a look that indicated Tom was out of sight of Colonel Edward Lansdale. He could get in a world of trouble staking out an Air Force colonel, but it was worth the risk. It had to be. The man was up to something, and Tom wanted to know what it was, especially if it could drag his godfather Willoughby into the muck.

Twice in the last month, Tom saw Lansdale with the priest, Father Diaz—if that was the man's real name—and Tom had finally coerced Candy Man to slip and tell him the man used at least two more aliases. Why would a priest need an alias? Tom had gone so far as to attend mass at the man's church, but he'd found nothing amiss there. The man—or priest—appeared as devout as any other Catholic priest Tom had encountered. Except this priest seemed to have ties to US authorities. But there was something more to it.

Tom and his men had followed Father Diaz a few times and watched him meet with his attorney Ferdinand Marcos twice. They exchanged thick rectangular envelopes, which Tom could only believe contained money.

Snake lifted a finger, then casually rubbed the left side of his nose.

Tom looked in that direction. Lansdale stepped out of the Philippine government building, looking all around him as he did. *Why so worried, Colonel? Who do you think is watching you?* A satisfied grin touched Tom's lips. At least the Colonel's instincts were sharp.

Lansdale walked the length of the building, and Tom fell in about fifty yards behind him, across the street. Tom pulled his fedora low on his brow and turned up his jacket collar. He could be any man walking home after work.

Ahead of him, Lansdale cut down a side street. Tom hustled across the road, throwing up a hand to pause traffic as a man on a bicycle swerved to miss him.

"Watch where you go!" the man yelled, shaking his fist.

Tom jogged onward without looking back, but he saw Snake shaking his head and grinning from farther up the block, past the alley Lansdale had entered. When Tom reached the corner, he sauntered around it, not wanting to run headlong into Lansdale, but not wanting to lose him, either. He spotted the man at the end of the block, his head bent close to Father Diaz's. Tom's steps faltered.

He looked around for a covert vantage point, but the littered alley wasn't as busy as the street.

Quickly Tom stepped into a doorway. A few feet away, a dirty newspaper lay on the ground, and Tom snatched it up. He opened the paper and leaned against the doorframe, a local resident stepping out for fresh air while he caught up on the news.

Tom peered over the top of the paper, watched as Diaz placed his hand on Lansdale's shoulder. He surely wasn't a kindly priest offering comfort to one of his parishioners. And Diaz wasn't wearing his cassock, but was dressed in a barong tagalong, the ever-present gold cross around his neck. He, too, could be any man. Diaz looked up, and Tom quickly ducked behind the paper. Chuck Yeager's face and the Bell X-1 rocket plane graced the page he'd opened, news of the US Air Force pilot's breach of the sound barrier finally reaching the Philippines. Tom checked the date on the paper. It was over a month old. No matter. He stepped forward a few inches, just in time to see Diaz pull a large, square, paper-wrapped packet from beneath his shirt and hand it to Lansdale. While the two were still standing close enough to embrace, Lansdale slid the packet into his coat. The priest wasn't an informant, at least in the traditional sense, Tom knew. Whatever information and material he and Lansdale were passing back and forth couldn't be traded in public. Could Tom trust Willoughby enough to talk to him about this?

Tom glanced down the block the way he'd come. He didn't see Snake, but he knew he was there just the same. When he looked back toward Lansdale, his breath caught. The two men had finished whatever transaction they'd made, and Father Diaz was heading toward him at a fast walk. Tom folded the newspaper, tucked it under his arm and walked back the way he came, turning sharply at the corner and entering the first business he encountered—a hardware shop.

Tom ducked into a row of paint cans near the front of the store, standing close enough to the dusty windows to see out, but not close enough to be seen, he hoped.

A short man with an explosion of dark hair spoke from behind Tom. "Hep you, sir?" he said in a thick Tagalog accent.

Tom startled. "No," he said in English, then switched to Tagalog. "No. Ahh, yes. I—I'm just looking."

"What you looking for? I hep."

"No, that's okay. I'll know when I see it." Tom glanced out the window. He fingered a display of electrical tape, picking up a roll, but not looking at it. Out the window, Father Diaz crossed the street. Tom dropped the roll of tape and hustled out the door.

"Sir? Sir?" the sales clerk called after him. "Come again!"

Tom didn't turn back, but crossed the street, falling in behind Snake, who already tailed Diaz. "Go get the car," he said quietly. "Bring it around."

Within a block, Ricky stepped out from a café and followed Diaz until the priest stopped, glanced around, then opened his car door, slid in and drove off.

Snake pulled up beside Ricky and motioned for him to get in. They drove back to the FBI office.

As soon as they settled in their office, Ricky offered a yellow envelope to Tom. "Urgent message arrived for you."

Tom slid his finger under the envelope flap, and pulled out a telegram. He opened his mouth, closed it, then smacked the paper against hand. "Unbelievable."

"What is it?" asked Ricky.

"Holy Cow! I can't believe this! We have travel plans."

Snake glanced up from his notes. "What's going on?"

Ricky shrugged.

Tom looked at neither man. "Hong Kong."

"What about it?" asked Snake.

"That's where we're going."

Ricky and Snake looked at each other, then Ricky touched Tom's arm. "Care to clue us in on why, boss?"

Tom looked at a calendar. "All I know is that I have to be sitting by the phone in—" He checked his watch. "Twenty minutes. Then I'll receive a call from Hoover with specifics about our morning trip to Hong Kong."

"Morn—" Ricky couldn't finish his sentence.

Snake grinned. "Chinese food. Yum."

Tom hung up the phone and looked at Snake, then Ricky. "We need to pack."

"Can you tell us more?" Ricky asked. "You know, the why and how of this trip?"

Tom sat down and propped his elbows on his knees, clasping his hands together. "There's a hotel heiress in Hong Kong who is in the process of building a new hotel there. She's using Federal Reserve Bonds to finance it."

Snake sucked his breath through his teeth. "And?"

"And those bonds are illegal."

"Ah," Ricky said. "Well, where did she get them? And how?"

Tom jabbed his finger in the air. "That's what we're going to find out. They know—we know—that she obtained them from an investor, but we have to find out who that person is."

Snake shook his head. "What about Candy Man? We're supposed to meet with him tomorrow night, see if he has obtained more information for you on Taruc."

Tom's shoulders sagged. "I know. I know." He pinched his forefinger and thumb together. "We're this close to finding out what Taruc has up his sleeve, and now we're being sent away." He shook his head.

"Why us, boss?" Ricky asked. "Can't Hoover send someone else?"

"He instructed me not to disagree with his decision. Said my language skills could get me further than anyone else they could send over there on short notice."

"Say we're leaving in the morning?"

Tom nodded, then stared toward the window. "Snake, can you reach Candy Man tonight, let him know we can't meet tomorrow?"

"Yeah. Passed his lackey on the street a while ago while we were following the priest. He's probably still dallying around town." Snake headed for the door, then paused with his hand on the doorknob. "Hoover say anything else?"

"Yes," Tom said, his mouth twisting sideways. "He said once I got a look at that heiress, I'd thank him."

Chapter 13

November 14, 1947

Hong Kong

"LADIES AND GENTLEMEN, please put your seatbacks in the upright position, and prepare to land. Thank you for flying Philippine Airlines." As the stewardess repeated the instructions in Tagalog, Chinese and a few other languages, the plane's drag pulled back. Tom chuckled. He understood the instructions in each of the languages—even though the stewardess had fractured the Mandarin dialect. Through the window, in place of ocean, spots of land grew larger beneath them.

Snake spun the cylinder on his revolver.

Tom scowled at Snake. "Put that thing away."

Snake grinned and snapped shut the cylinder. "You got it, boss."

Ricky shook his head at Tom. "He checks those bullets at least a dozen times a day." He looked at Snake. "You know, most people count on their fingers, not on their bullets."

"Okay, that's enough," Tom said. "These British MI-6 agents are known for their professional demeanor. We don't want to look like a bunch of yahoos, so get it together before we disembark."

Snake sobered and holstered his gun.

"I still don't understand why Hoover wanted us to come all this way for a day or two, just to question this woman." Ricky slid a suit jacket over his Hawaiian shirt. "Why can't the MI-6 agent interview her and just tell us what she said?"

Tom peered out the airplane window as they taxied to a stop ever so slowly. "Hoover doesn't tell me why. He gives the orders, we carry them out."

Attendants pushed over a rolling staircase, and within a few moments, the airplane's side door opened.

Tom noticed first that the MI-6 agent's suit must have cost a small fortune. Impeccably tailored, the black material practically glimmered in the fading afternoon light. What struck him as odd, though, was the suit looked like it had been slept in.

The dark-haired man thrust forward a hand. "Special Agent Thomas Warren?"

Tom nodded and shook the man's hand.

"MI-6 Anthony Middleton." The man met Tom's eyes with a piecing stare. "Welcome to Hong Kong."

Middleton repeated his name-and-title introduction with both Love and McCoy.

Snake shook the man's hand and said, "Folks call me *Snake*."

Tom turned his head to hide his smile.

"We needed you here yesterday. The delay has already damaged our ability to question the heiress. Please hurry. Our car is waiting." Agent Middleton walked away from the trio.

Tom glanced over his shoulder, but realized an attendant had already loaded their few bags onto a cart and waited to follow. He shrugged and fell into step behind Middleton.

Inside the car, Middleton quickly debriefed the men, his heavy British accent a distraction. "The lady's name is Isabella Scarborough. British, although I'd say she has some Chinese in her, if you know what I mean." He continued, not explaining. "Comes from money, and lots of it. All right?" He raised a thick eyebrow at his American guests, then continued. "I warn you, do not let her beauty distract you from your mission, Agent Warren. She—"

"Please. Call me *Tom*." He scowled. "And I don't typically drool over pretty ladies when I have a job to do, sir."

Middleton met Tom's eyes without wavering. "This woman eats men for lunch. Especially handsome men, and you're quite the handsome lad."

Tom wanted to say something, but nothing sounded right.

"She uses her looks as both a tool and a weapon. Respectfully, sir, it is my job to tell you this, just as it's your job to keep a level head."

Tom pressed his lips together. "Got it."

"I've spoken with Miss Scarborough, and I believe she will cooperate with you—that is, if she likes you. You must befriend her, but remember that she is right powerful, and if she distrusts you, she will shut down and tell you nothing. Right?"

Tom stared at Middleton, but didn't speak. Who did this man think he was, anyway? Pompous Brit. He turned to stare out the window.

As Middleton digressed into the logistics of the hotel heiress's daily routine, Tom stared out the window. A familiar-looking man wearing a gray suit headed out of an airline terminal. Tom leaned forward, pressing his face to the glass. Surely he was seeing things. Surely—"Stop!" he called. He jabbed his finger against the window. "Stop the car. That's him!"

"Who?" Middleton asked.

Snake and Ricky leaned to peer out the window where Tom pointed. The driver slowed, but when Middleton shook his head, he didn't stop the car.

"The man who knocked me down. There, in the gray suit."

"Yep," Snake said, sucking breath through his teeth. "That's him all right. What's he doing in Hong Kong?"

"Stop the car!" Tom ordered.

Middleton shook his head, and the driver again accelerated. "No time. You're a wee bit late already. And because of that, we had to let the heiress out of jail—we could no longer hold her. She is free, so we have no leverage. All righty?"

Tom clenched his teeth and sank back into the seat. He wasn't sure how much more of this man's attitude he was willing to take.

"We will be questioning Miss Scarborough in her penthouse, instead of our own holding area. You understand this gives her an advantage."

Tom met the man's disdainful stare. "I didn't ask for an advantage. I didn't come all this way to leave without the information I came for, so don't worry about me. I'll be just fine."

Snake cleared his throat and leaned forward. He flipped the edge of a photo with his thumbnail. "Excuse me, Agent Middleton. Have you seen this man? That's who I think we just saw."

Tom glanced at the picture as Middleton took it from Snake's hand. It was the gray-suited man.

Middleton studied the photo and handed it back to Snake. "No. I haven't seen that gent before, I don't believe. All right?"

Snake leaned closer. "You've never seen him before?"

"No. Who is he?"

Snake pocketed the photo. "We're not sure. He just keeps popping up in places we wouldn't expect to see him. Like here. In Hong Kong."

Middleton tilted his head to one side. "No idea. He looks Chinese to me. Perhaps this is where he lives. Right-o?"

Tom offered an easy smile. "You're probably right."

An hour later, Tom and his men stood with Middleton by the concierge desk at the heiress's hotel. After a moment, a man wearing a hotel uniform stepped out of the elevator and walked up to Middleton. "Miss Scarborough will see you now."

Tom nodded to Ricky, who took a seat across from the elevators in the hotel lobby.

Middleton, Tom and Snake followed the hotel attendant onto the elevator. The attendant inserted a long golden key into a special lock, and the elevator slowly rose to the penthouse floor.

Tom was no stranger to opulence, yet the sumptuous affluence that surrounded him when he stepped off the elevator into the penthouse foyer caught him off guard. Gold-flecked Italian marble created swirled designs in light and dark browns that shone beneath the elephant-sized crystal chandelier. The wall surrounding the massive double doors to Miss Scarborough's home was made of tufted lambskin leather. Tom's fingers twitched as he stifled the urge to stroke the wall.

The hotel attendant pressed a golden button set into the wall, and a lyrical chime floated through the cavernous entryway. Immediately, both heavy doors swung open silently, as if weightless. The attendant stepped aside, and a man wearing a tailored silk suit stood just inside the door.

"Agent Middleton." The man's voice was emotionless.

Tom and Middleton followed the man inside, while Snake took a seat on the high-backed leather bench in the foyer.

"Miss Scarborough will be right with you," the man Tom assumed to be a butler said.

Late afternoon sunlight shone through floor-to-ceiling windows, giving ethereal movement to the graceful nudes and artistic statuary poised throughout the room. Paintings Tom recognized as originals decorated silk-covered walls, giving the room a museum-like quality. "How does she keep the sunlight from damaging her artwork?" Tom whispered to Middleton.

"Not my concern, right?" Middleton eyelids flickered heavy with boredom.

Tom shrugged, his lips parting of their own accord as the woman floated into the room. Middleton's description of beauty didn't apply to this woman. She was exquisite. Tom couldn't help but let his eyes drink in her splendor. Coppery red hair dropped silky straight from her scalp, but cascaded in curls around her flawless, delicate face and shoulders.

Isabella Scarborough wore a peach satin dressing gown that hugged her curves, its full, flowing skirt trailing behind her as she walked. The gown was slit high on her thigh, revealing long ivory legs ending in high-heeled marabou mules that seemed never to touch the ground. She didn't so much walk as dance across the floor toward Tom and Middleton.

Tom knew his mouth hung open, tried to close it, but couldn't. As Miss Scarborough drew close, he could smell her, the light scent of honey and spice wafting ahead of her. He wanted to lift his nose, close his eyes and inhale. She smelled like heaven.

"Good day, gentlemen." Her voice was a gentle as a spring rain, soft, melodious. She offered her hand to Middleton, then to Tom.

"Miss Scarborough, allow me to introduce Special Agent Thomas Warren of the United States Federal Bureau of Investigation."

Tom took the woman's hand, lifted it, nearly making the mistake of kissing it, instead of shaking it. He caught himself in time, but felt heat rush into his face. "It's a pleasure to meet you, Miss Scarborough."

"Please," she said, holding Tom's gaze a moment too long, "call me Izzy."

Izzy. The last thing Izzy appeared to be was powerful. She was a fragile flower, delicate beyond human possibility. Tom wanted to protect her, save her. Hold her. Hug her.

Middleton grabbed his arm and squeezed. "Special Agent Warren is here to complete our interrogation, Miss Scarborough. Is there some place we might talk privately?"

Isabella Scarborough gave Middleton an amused smile and waved one hand languidly through the air. "My entire home is private, Mr. Middleton." She slipped a hand into the crook of Tom's arm. "However, if I'm going to be *interrogated* by Thomas—may I call you Thomas?—then I wish to speak with him alone."

Middleton opened his mouth, closed it, then opened it again. "I don't think—I believe I should be present for this interrogation, all right?"

Whether it was his own sense of masculine competition or simply the nearness of this woman, Tom wasn't sure, but he felt himself stand straighter, surer. "*Interrogation* is such a strong word. Actually, Izzy, I'd just like to chat with you for a moment. A little give-and-take, if you will."

"Oooh, I'd like that." She lifted one perfectly arched bronze eyebrow. "Especially the *take* part."

Middleton cleared his throat. "Right. Where shall we talk, Miss Scarborough?"

"You," she said, pointing a burgundy-painted nail at Middleton, "may wait over there, while Thomas and I talk in my room."

Tom chuckled. "I'd prefer to talk elsewhere, if you don't mind." He played along with her flirtatious game and gave his best teasing smile. "I might get distracted if we talk in your room."

She tossed her long mane of coppery-red curls over one shoulder. "Very well, then." Izzy strolled toward a seating nook in view of the main room, then sat on a dark red satin divan and crossed her legs, the split in her gown revealing the full length of her slender thigh.

She was tiny, obviously part-Chinese by the slant of her dark eyes, but the lightness of her skin and hair suggested some Irish ancestry as well.

Tom forced himself to lock onto her eyes. "I won't keep you long, Miss Sca—Izzy. I understand you've had a rather harrowing few days."

She waved off Tom's comment. "It was nothing. Just a misunderstanding on the part of Mr. Middleton, if you will." She smiled, her white teeth shining like pearls. She leaned forward, and the front of her dressing gown fell open, exposing the curve of her ivory breasts. "Must we get right into the questioning, Thomas? After being detained for two days, I'm a little . . . restless." The delicacy of her soft voice hung in the air, absorbing all oxygen it touched.

Tom shifted, struggling for breath. Her eyes boldly roved his body. Women often appraised him with their eyes, but he'd never encountered one as brash as Isabella Scarborough. Heat flowed through his chest and neck and into his face. He tugged at his collar, which suddenly felt too tight.

Izzy lifted a hand toward him. "Uncomfortable, Thomas? Perhaps a bit too warm? Here, let me take your jacket."

Tom scooted backward on his chair. "That's okay, thank you. I'm fine." He glanced across the large front room, where Middleton stood in front of a painting, pretending to examine it as he eavesdropped. The man scowled at him.

"Let's get right to it, shall we?" Tom forced his mind to clear, forced his body to detach from the spell Izzy wove. He had a job to do. "You had in your possession a half a million dollars in Federal Reserve Bonds. *Illegal* FRBs. I'd like to know where you got them, please."

Izzy tilted her head downward, looked up at Tom through long eyelashes. "You said *please*. I like a gentleman with good manners."

Tom pressed his lips together. Her game had grown old. "They were a loan, yes? From an investor? Where did you get them?"

The woman feigned a yawn. "All this business and no pleasure. It makes for a very dull boy, Thomas."

"What do you want? Let's put our cards on the table, Miss Scarborough, because I don't have time for games."

Izzy lifted her face toward him. "Finally. A man who knows what he wants and speaks with authority. I like it." She leaned forward again, her dressing gown slipping off one shoulder, coming dangerously close to exposing her breast. "I'll tell you everything you want to know." She stared at him. "Everything. Anything. But first. . . . " She trailed her fingers across the back of his hand. "First, come into my bed. You can have the information you want, but I must get something in return."

"Ma'am, I'm sorry, but—"

"You asked me what I wanted. I want you." Her pout was both endearing and aggravating.

Tom tried to conjure an image of Judy in his mind, but couldn't. Their phone calls, difficult to make overseas, often ended in disconnections with no way to reconnect. They'd tried to talk weekly, despite the expense Tom gladly bore, but then their calls grew further apart, and now Tom realized it had been at least five weeks since he'd talked to her. And several months since he'd been with a woman.

His eyes found Izzy's milky white neck, traveled down to the hollow of her throat where her pulse fluttered, then down to the creamy swell that disappeared beneath peach satin. His tactile senses were on high alert, and he ached to reach out and touch her.

Middleton coughed.

Tom looked up to see the man had drawn closer and now stood less than a few yards away. His brow had corrugated and his eyes narrowed. Tom's jaw tightened. Hoover had given him a mission, had sent him all the way to Hong Kong to retrieve information from this woman. How he obtained that information was up to him. Middleton be damned.

"You can wait in the hallway with McCoy," Tom said to Middleton. "Or downstairs with Agent Love, if you prefer." He turned and met Izzy's caramel-colored eyes. "Miss Scarborough and I would like to speak in private."

Middleton's mouth dropped open. He struggled to speak, finally stammering, "I don't think—"

"That's okay, Agent Middleton." Izzy batted her long eyelashes. "I don't need you to think." She gave him a moment to reflect on her words, then smiled sweetly. "Agent Warren and I have some personal business to attend to, and then we shall talk."

She moved her hand to wave Middleton away, but Tom grabbed her wrist in mid-air. "Information first. Satisfaction later." He held her wrist tight.

Izzy's breath caught, but then she let out a long, slow breath. "Promise?" She slowly licked her lips.

Tom leaned toward her, his face hardly an inch from hers, and let his eyes devour her mouth. "Tell me what I want to know, and I am yours for the evening."

"I must—" said Middleton, but Tom held up a hand, silencing him.

"Dismissed, Agent Middleton," Tom said.

Middleton stomped out of the room like a child, and Tom slid a hand into Izzy's silky curls. A soft moan escaped her lips, and she leaned in to kiss Tom, but he pulled back and smiled. "Information first."

A quick flash of anger lit her eyes, then quickly disappeared. "Fine. Let's get this out of the way." She pulled closed the neckline of her dressing gown and sat straighter. "What, exactly, do you want to know?"

Tom leaned backward and squared his shoulders. "The FRBs. Who is the investor who gave them to you?"

"My banker. Next question."

"We know that. But your banker got them from the investor, yes?"

"That's right."

"Who is the investor?"

Izzy looked around the room as if looking for an escape.

"We can play cat and mouse if you want, Izzy, or we can get this out of the way and spend the rest of the evening any way you wish. It's up to you, but personally, I can think of other things I'd rather be doing right now, so let's get this over with, shall we?"

She turned her gaze back to Tom and smiled. "You're right, of course. I always did love a smart man." She lightly cleared her throat. "The FRBs came from H.H. Kung."

"Kung? You are sure about this?"

Izzy nodded. "Of course I am certain."

Tom took a deep breath. "After their drawn out war with Japan—well, I never realized the man was still that wealthy."

"You have no idea, do you?" Izzy's soft voice purred over the reprimand. "Chiang Kai-shek and T.V. Soong used the government's banks to buy the government's bonds when Soong was Finance Minister of China. They also extended loans to the government this way. Pure financial incest." She shook her head but offered a slight smile.

"So," said Tom, "you're telling me they used bank instruments to do private business? The US Federal Reserve Bonds are to remain in the banking system; they are not negotiable instruments. The Chinese were to use them to finance their war with Japan. "

"Exactly. But Chiang Kai-shek and T.V. Soong didn't always get along. Sometimes they argued. T.V. had money—FRBs, plenty of gold—but had little political power to make anything happen. Soong's family made Chiang a wealthy man, and now Soong wants his pay back. Chiang had the power, but didn't have as much money. H.H. Kung got along well with both of them, so he became the middleman."

Tom rubbed his chin. "But Kung was finance minister, wasn't he? Why was it so easy to influence him?"

"It's sad, really. I don't think H.H. knew what he was getting into. He is from one of the prominent families of Old China—he *claims* he is a direct descendent of Confucius." She shrugged tiny shoulders. "Regardless, he is exceedingly rich and quite intellectual. All he hopes for is to get away from a bad situation."

It surprised Tom to see her eyes puddle. He wanted to reach out his hand and touch her, but she quickly straightened, regaining control.

"He wants a way out. Truly. He looked for options. He thought—I thought—we figured by him investing in my new hotel, it would give him a way out of their mess. He loaned me the FRBs—not real money, anyway, so no risk involved—and if they were accepted as collateral, then I would repay him with cash, and he'd be clean." She shrugged, but held her delicate chin steady, resolute.

Tom looked away. If Kung truly wanted away from Chiang and Soong, then perhaps he would be willing to cooperate in exchange for leniency and freedom. He looked back at Izzy. "I want to talk to him. I want to talk to H.H. Kung."

Izzy stared at him for almost a minute before she spoke. "You will have to offer him protection from the Chinese Communists. Speaking to you will endanger him, perhaps to the point of losing his life. He is a marked man as long as Chairman Mao is alive."

"If I can offer that, if I can guarantee his protection, will he speak to me?"

Izzy folded her hands in her lap. "I believe he will, yes. H.H. wants out of the Chinese civil war. He wants to make money in the free world. He wants to get away from Soong and Chiang."

"Can you contact him now?"

A delicate chuckle escaped her small lips. "No, not right now. He is . . . *away*, let us say. It may take a while, weeks, maybe a month or longer, but I can arrange something."

Tom shook his head. "That won't help me. I have to be on a plane tomorrow—the day after, at the latest."

"Impossible. I can't reach him that soon."

A roadblock. But Tom had acquired a name for Hoover. H.H. Kung. That's what he'd come for, and it would have to be enough. He glanced at his watch. "I can't stick around that long. But I don't have to be on that flight until tomorrow." He let his eyes roam her body, settle in her caramel gaze. "That means I have hours to kill. Any ideas as to how I should spend them?"

Izzy leaned toward in a painfully slow, fluid motion, her mouth hovering over his forehead, his eyes, his nose, his mouth.

Tom reached for her, but she stood and shrugged out of her gown, allowing it to cascade into a satin puddle at her feet. She stepped forward, wearing only her high heeled shoes, grabbed Tom's tie and pulled him to his feet, leading him as if by a leash toward her bedroom.

Chapter 14

February 9, 1948
Montalban Gorge, Manila, Philippines

TOM PEERED THROUGH the dusty windshield of Snake's cherry red Chevy as it navigated the brutal curves and steep inclines of the winding dirt road. "Are you sure this is the right road? It doesn't look that well-traveled." The road—no more than a path, really—was supposed to lead them to a site where men were actively digging for gold.

Ricky leaned forward and draped his arms over the front seat of the car. "Candy Man gave very specific directions. Said they sometimes drag heavy branches behind their trucks so they'll wipe away any sign of tire treads."

"That's really smart." Snake deftly navigated the deep ruts. "He said this was where that Chinese guy we were looking for was digging. But I still don't like it. It's kind of creepy."

Ricky chuckled. "You're just scared you might see a ghost." He playfully shoved Snake's shoulder, causing his hand to slip from the steering wheel.

"Hey, watch it!" Snake scowled. "You only say that because you've never seen a ghost before. Well I *have*. And let me tell you, it's enough to make your skin crawl." Despite his size, the big man shivered and his eyes grew round like a child's. "You heard what Candy Man said. That priest is a ghost-man."

Tom turned to hide his grin, but his serious composure resurfaced when he saw the three papaya trees forming a triangle. "Hey, stop the car."

Snake did as he was told.

"Pull over there, near those bushes, between the papaya trees." Tom pointed to an area of dense foliage.

"I don't know. This place gives me the creeps." Snake shook his head. "Hey, boss, let's grab some extra speed loaders and bullets."

Tom chuckled. "Well, get over it. According to Candy Man, we should be about four hundred meters—about a quarter of a mile—from the dig site."

"Let me back the car in, so we'll be in a position for a quick escape." Snake said.

Ricky punched his shoulder. "You're just plain weird, you know that?"

Snake's mouth twisted to one side, then he parked, taking the keys and dropping them into his pocket. "Guess you're right." The three stepped out of the bright red car.

"Don't you think this monster is going to stand out?" Ricky motioned around at the surrounding greenness. "I mean, even in the bushes, it looks like a giant poppy."

"Yeah." Tom sighed. "Grab some brush, and let's cover it."

After a few moments of tugging at surprisingly strong plants, Snake pulled out his knife. The others followed suit, and soon they had the car adequately covered.

Ricky wiped the late afternoon heat from his brow. "Now I suppose we have to hike up that damn mountain."

They all looked up the steep incline at the rugged path.

Tom shrugged. "Suppose so. Let's get started."

As they approached the operation, the ground vibrated with the sound of heavy equipment. Tom waved for Snake and Ricky to fall in behind him. When they neared the clearing, he squatted and peered through heavy brush at an excavation site.

"Any sign of that weird Chinese guy?" Ricky whispered.

Tom squinted. "I don't think so. They look—"He turned and faced his comrades. "They're Japanese!"

Ricky and Snake dropped to the ground and wiggled closer to the dig site. They too gazed at the site before them.

About fifteen Japanese men worked a variety of heavy equipment and pick axes to dig into the rocky soil. One of the men wearing a khaki shirt and pants motioned to another wearing a black turtleneck. The man in the turtleneck picked up the binoculars that hung from his neck and looked through them—in the direction of Tom and his men. He nodded at the first man.

"I think we've been spotted," Ricky whispered.

The first man blew a whistle. All work stopped. The men jumped off equipment and took cover behind it. Some men who were loading gold into trucks dropped the gold, pulled handguns from waistbands, and fired at the agents.

"Holy shit!" Snake rolled behind a boulder and grabbed for his .38 Special. He and Ricky shot toward those firing. One of the Japanese men grabbed his shoulder and toppled over.

Two workers jumped into trucks.

Ricky blew on the top of his gun. "We scared them off," he said. "They're leaving."

Tom squinted toward the late afternoon sun. "Stay under cover. They're heading this—"

Before he could finish his sentence, a shot sounded and the dirt erupted a few feet in front of Tom. All three agents aimed handguns at the two oncoming trucks and fired.

Another half-dozen or so men produced rifles and pistols, and shot toward Tom, Snake and Ricky.

"We've been set up!" Ricky yelled.

"Cover!"

The three jumped behind more substantial trees. Bullets zinged around them as the trucks drove right through the spot where they'd stood just seconds before.

Instead of coming back for another run toward Tom and his men, the trucks bounced to the dirt road and headed down the mountain.

Bullets continued to fly around them.

"How do we get out of here?" Ricky asked. "We've got no cover if we head back to the car."

"I'm going after those trucks. They can't outrun me in my car." Snake opened his gun and quickly replaced the bullets with one in his speed loader. "Stay covered! I'll be back for you."

Before Tom could respond, Snake darted from behind the brush and ran down the slope, ducking in and out of palmetto stands lining the path as he angled back toward the car. Tom looked at Ricky and shrugged a shoulder, and the two of them ran out from opposite sides of the scrub brush as fresh gunfire sounded from the hill above. Ricky and Tom continued to return gunfire. Two Japanese men ran toward them; Ricky immediately killed both. Two more Japanese men emerged from the cave and crisscrossed to a closer position.

Tom shouted to Ricky, "Let's get out of here while we can. Head back to the road and try to catch up with Snake. Otherwise, they're going to encircle us and we're going to run out of ammo."

Ricky rose and fired two more times, then shouted, "Let me reload first!" He pulled out a speed loader quickly open his .38 dumped the spentbullets and quickly replaced them.

Tom fired steadily. "Hurry." He waited until Ricky had snapped the cylinder into place.

"Okay," Ricky said. "I'm going to cross the road. Then you follow. Okay?"

"Yeah. Be careful."

Ricky zigged and zagged the gunfire as Tom rose and randomly fired on the Japanese positions. Once Ricky was across the road and behind a tree, Tom ran straight across the road. He'd rather stake his life on his speed than his zigging and zagging ability.

Once on the other side, both breathed a sigh of relief. They now stood on the forested side of the road and could easily see anyone who tried to cross the road. "Let's get out of here," Tom said. Instead of staying close to the road, they moved a bit deeper into the heavy underbrush, but tried to go as quickly as they could down the steep incline. Palm thorns and sharp edges of the saw palmettos tore into their arms and sliced their hands. Still better than gunfire slashing their skin.

By the time they reached the area where Snake's car had been hidden, the gunfire above them had stopped.

"Looks like Snake is in pursuit," Ricky said.

Tom sighed. "I wish he'd just waited for us. I think I'd rather just get out of this mess and think up a plan before taking on a mob of armed Japanese."

"What now, boss?"

"The only place Snake could've gone was down this path, so let's just follow it until we find him—or civilization, whichever comes first."

Nearly a mile down the mountain, Tom stopped and leaned against an oak tree to catch his breath. The gunshots had long since faded away. He looked around, his eyes sharp and his ears attuned for any sound that someone might be following them. His breath came in gasps and sounded too loud, like a great rush of wind, and he willed it to slow. When he breathed easier, he held his breath, listening carefully. Nothing but sounds of the forest.

"I don't think they followed us," Ricky said.

"The man in the turtleneck," Tom said. "The one at the site. He was Sasakawa Ryoichi." He rubbed his stinging hands. "And the man in the khakis was Komada Yoshio."

Ricky stared at Tom. "You sure?"

"Yes. I was sure back there, but it wasn't a good time to discuss it." Tom swatted at gnats. "They're Yakuza."

"I know. But why would Candy Man send us into the midst of a heavily armed organized crime mob?"

"Only one reason I can think of." Tom scowled. "Come on. Let's find Snake and get the hell out of here."

Almost two hours later, the two neared the bottom of the mountain. Afternoon daylight had turned to evening dusk, and they now walked closer to the road under cover of the wooded darkness.

"You don't think we missed the car, do you?" Ricky whispered.

Tom shook his head. "No. Snake must have chased them farther then we figured. I don't know how they could have outrun *that* car."

They walked another three hundred yards, and Ricky pointed ahead. "Hey! There it is. There's the car."

Below them was a widening in the road, a relatively flat section where a vehicle could turn around or pass another vehicle. In the center of this widening was Snake's Chevy Town Sedan.

Though exhausted, Tom felt a surge of energy and he pushed faster through the heavy underbrush. As he drew close, he threw out his arm to hold Ricky back. "Wait. Something isn't right."

Ricky breathed heavily behind him. "What?"

"The tires are flat."

"It might be a trap." Ricky shielded his eyes from the setting sun.

A sick feeling gnawed at Tom's gut. "Where's Snake?"

The two remained in the dense growth until they drew parallel to the car. "He's in there," Ricky said. "Looks like he's asleep."

Tom held up a hand. "Listen."

The two remained motionless for almost a minute. Then they pulled out their guns.

"I think we're alone, but proceed with caution," he whispered. "You circle around to the left of the car, and I'll approach from the right." Tom slowly made his way down the bank toward the dirt road, looking all around him as he descended. In the last dregs of fading sunlight, he saw Snake's hand on the steering wheel. He motioned to Ricky. When he reached the last bush that could give him any semblance of cover, he paused and listened, peering up and down the road for any sign of the Yakuza. The early evening remained quiet, and he saw no one.

Tom reached the passenger car door and pecked his knuckle on the window. He grabbed the door handle, realizing Snake hadn't moved. When he opened the door, the rusty stench of copper told him all he didn't want to know. A moan caught in his throat, and he turned and gagged.

Ricky opened the driver's door and leaned into the car, a sob breaking in his chest. He reached in and tried to pull Snake toward him. Snake's throat was gashed so deeply the poor man's head rocked, as if it might fall off his neck. Ricky took out his knife and cut his hands free, then cradled Snake against his chest, gently rocking him as he would a wounded child.

Tom's throat tightened and his eyes burned. He swallowed hard and tried to compose himself. He moved into the passenger seat and put a hand on Ricky's shoulder, gripping him as if life force could flow out of his body, through Ricky's and into Snake.

After a few minutes, he turned to Ricky "When we get out of this, we're going to pay a visit to Candy Man."

Ricky nodded.

"One of us has to walk out of here for help and the other has to stay here with Snake . . . this is now a crime scene."

Ricky's chin quivered. "I'll stay."

Hours later, when Tom returned with help, they learned that every rumor they'd heard about how vicious and heartless the Japanese Yakuza could be was true. Mud and leaves smeared on Snake's clothes proved that he'd been dragged from the car before he was killed. His legs were broken in several places, and his hands had been crushed and tied to the steering wheel. A message to Tom—and anyone associated with him—that they'd come too close and must stay away from the gold burial sites.

The medical staff slid Snake's body from his prized automobile. After Tom watched his bodyguard, his compatriot, his friend, loaded into the medical vehicle, he leaned over the ditch, his body trembling, and vomited.

Chapter 15

Tuesday Morning, February 10, 1948
Manila, Philippines

RICKY ARRIVED AT Snake's apartment almost thirty minutes prior to the time he was supposed to meet Tom. To his surprise, Tom was already there. With a deep sigh, Ricky shuffled up to the front door and knocked.

"Open," Tom called.

Ricky walked into the small apartment. To his surprise, the area was well kept, everything neatly in its place. Tom sat in a chair next to the radio, staring into space.

"You all right?"

Tom nodded. "Just want to get this over with."

"Me, too. I'll take the bedroom."

Tom shrugged. "Glad you want the bedroom. I'd feel weird going through another guy's personal stuff."

"The whole thing is weird, and the sooner we get done, the sooner we can go pay a visit to Candy Man." Ricky took three shuffling steps across the small living area to the door leading to the bedroom. He scanned the room. Above the bed was an oil painting of the ocean at sunset. A memory stabbed Ricky's heart. Years ago—not long after they'd first met—Snake had pulled him aside and said, "Look, if anything ever happens to me—if I don't get off these islands on my own two feet—look behind the painting of the ocean. Got it?" Nothing more had ever been said.

Was that the picture he'd referred to?

Ricky filled his lungs with oxygen, leaned over the headboard and lifted the painting off the nail. He flipped it over and stared. Taped to the back was an envelope. He dropped the painting onto the bed and removed the envelope. Should he call for Tom before opening it? Probably not. Snake had told him, not Tom.

Ricky opened the envelope. It contained a photograph. He stared at it for a few moments, then, without moving an inch, yelled, "Tom! Hey, Tom! Get in here!"

"What?" Tom hollered back. "I'm busy!"

"No. Get in here."

Tom appeared in the doorway with a growl. "What's so blasted important?"

"Look at this."

"What's that?" Tom asked.

"A picture. Look at it closely."

⊶⊷

Tom stared at the photograph. In it, Willoughby, alongside a young, clean-shaven Snake, stood in front of a brig, a big grin on his face, with prisoners standing behind him.

"Willoughby?" Tom asked.

"Yes. Go on."

"Snake?" Tom carried the photograph to the window, then squinted. "Is that Snake? With Willoughby? Why would Snake be with Willoughby?"

"Your guess is as good as mine, boss. Keep looking."

Tom studied the picture. "Wow. Is that Candy Man?" he whispered.

"Yes. Keep looking."

"Taruc? Alejandrino? And, who's that?"

"Beats me. Never saw the guy."

"But why would . . . ?" Tom flipped the photo over. On the back, in Snake's unique print, was written, "February 1945, first MP arrest with Brigadier General Charles Willoughby. Taruc, Alejandrino, Candy Man and Cayanan."

Tom almost dropped the picture. He returned to the front and looked again at the prisoners behind Snake.

"Snake and Willoughby worked together?"

"Looks like it. Pictures don't lie."

"Why didn't anyone tell me?" Heat crawled up Tom's face. Willoughby's report omitted the fact that Luis Taruc and Candy Man had been arrested after MacArthur's return to the Philippines at the beginning of 1945. There were no notes on their arrest, interrogation, why they were released. *Where was the documentation? On the first day in the FBI office, Willoughby had said this guy—Candy Man—would "sing like a canary." Did he sing then? Where are the notes? What did Taruc say? What did Candy Man say? What did the others?*

"Boss?"

Tom handed the photo to Ricky.

Ricky flipped it over and studied as Tom had, then whistled lowly.

"Who would have interrogation these men?" Tom asked. "Neither Willoughby nor MacArthur would just let those yahoos walk out of there. What's going on here?"

Ricky shook his head. "Let's go chat with Candy Man."

"Ricky, we *are* going to 'chat' with Candy Man, but we're going to play dumb and we're going to get real *chummy* with him—if you know what I mean. Then we're going to start watching him. We were sent here to investigate the communists, which have led us to investigating the Huks, and based on this picture alone, we are missing some crucial information. It's time we start to fill in the blanks ourselves. Let's finish here, then go pay Candy Man a visit."

When they had finished collecting Snake's personal effects and placing them neatly into a box, Tom looked down at it, scratched his head and said, "Snake sure lived a simple life, didn't he?"

Ricky just looked at the box, then at Tom, then turned and walked out the door with Tom in slow pursuit. They walked to Tom's car, got in, and drove off toward Candy Man's. The two were unusually silent as they drove. Snake's absence was obvious to both.

Tom stared out the window, watching the morning activity on the streets of Manila. Suddenly he jerked around in his seat. "Since there were no notes in the briefing Willoughby gave me, it must be because he wasn't the one who interrogated these fine folks. And if not him, who? Who would have interrogated

Candy Man? Or Taruc? Think about it. MacArthur was on these islands for a decade before he had to evacuate because of the Japanese invasion. Who did he have here? Did he have local spies reporting to him?"

"What are you getting at, boss?"

"I don't know. I'm just thinking aloud. Something fishy is going on, and I just can't put my finger on it."

After a few more minutes, they arrived at Candy Man's home and parked out in front.

Ricky tightened his grip on the door handle. "I can't wait to get my hands on that Commie creep."

"Keep yourself under control." As they walked up to the door, Tom spoke under his breath. "Let me do the talking."

Ricky beat on the door so hard Tom thought it might come off the hinges.

"Who is it?" a voice from within asked.

"Me and Ricky," Tom said. "Let us in."

Candy Man opened the door slightly. "What do you want? You should not be seen here!"

"We have some bad news for you about your friend Snake."

"What news?"

"He is dead."

Candy Man opened the door. His coffee-colored face wrinkled with concern. He shook his head slightly. "Oh, no, how did it happen?"

Candy Man's acting skills weren't as sharp as they should be. Tom concentrated on breathing so as not to bash in the man's skull.

But not Ricky. He leaped past Tom, grabbed Candy Man by the throat and bounced him against the wall.

Candy Man's eyes bulged.

Tom jumped forward and put his hand on Ricky's shoulder. "C'mon now. We need this guy. He's going to give us something for his mistake. I want the name of the Chinese man and I want some information about him. Got it?"

Candy Man's face clouded. "I don't know anything." He shook his head and tears puddled in his eyes. "Please. I don't want to end up beheaded."

Ricky tightened his grip on Candy Man.

Tom pointed and wagged his index finger at Candy Man's nose. He was quite aware this was considered rude by Filipinos, but he intended it that way. "You will get me the information I want about the Chinese guy and about that priest or pretend priest or whoever he is." He lowered his voice. "And I want to know the structure of the Huks. I want more than the name of Luis Taruc. I want the power brokers." He took a step back. "You have one week to get me this information."

Ricky released Candy Man and stepped toward the door.

Tom followed him, but kept his eyes on Candy Man. "We will be back." Tom held his eyes on Candy Man, then looked at Ricky. "Let's go. Candy Man has some work to do, and we have to get Snake's personal effects to Clark Air Base."

As they drove off for the air base, Tom sighed deeply. "I have to find a way to tactfully ask Willoughby about that photo."

Chapter 16

February 16, 1948

Manila, Philippines

TOM SHOVED THE file folder into his desk drawer and pushed the drawer shut, then strolled to his office window and peered out. "He should be here soon."

"We taking him to lunch?" asked Ricky.

"If he gets here in time, sure."

Ricky stared at the floor, a hangdog expression on his face.

"He's going to be one of us now, you know."

Ricky didn't speak, didn't even blink. His eyes seemed to glaze over.

Tom pressed his lips together, then propped his elbows on his desk, steepling his fingers. "I miss Snake, too, you know."

Ricky slowly looked up, and the hurt in his eyes caused a lump in Tom's throat. "I know you do, boss." He stared out the window, his eyes seemingly unfocused on the world beyond the pane of glass. "It's just that . . . it feels like we're replacing him."

Tom pushed back from his desk. "No. No, that's not it at all. Snake can't be replaced." He chuckled softly. "That man was one of a kind. There'll never be another Robert McCoy. Ever." A sad smile pulled at his lips. "But the work goes on, Ricky. His position—his *job*—must be filled. We're putting Salvador Marino in Snake's old position, but there's no way in the world we're replacing our friendship, all that Snake meant to us." He looked out the window as well, his own gaze clouding with memory. "That's a position Snake held that no man can fill."

A sharp rap at the door brought Tom back to the present. He cleared his throat and straightened his tie, then nodded to Ricky.

Ricky stood and walked to the door. When he opened it, Marino walked in, hand outstretched.

"You must be Agent Richard Love. I'm Agent Salvador Marino." The man wore an air of authority as stately as he wore his black suit.

Ricky nodded and shook the man's hand, then nodded toward Tom. "This is Special Agent Tom Warren." When Marino walked toward Tom, again with hand outstretched, Ricky scowled.

Tom stood and shook hands, looking the man up and down. He was solidly built, though not as big as Snake. *Don't compare them.* He had more body padding than Ricky, whose surfer's body stayed muscled and lean, despite his ravenous appetite. "Have a seat." Tom waved to the chairs surrounding a round table. "Hoover said you'd be punctual."

Marino smiled. "Of course. What else did he say?"

Tom stared at the man a moment, then returned his smile. "Let's see . . . he said you were meticulous, efficient, and that when you dig for information, you leave no stone unturned."

The dark-haired man nodded. "That sounds like me, yes."

Tom picked up a pencil and slid it back and forth between his fingers. "Interesting choice of words. 'Dig for information. Leave no stone unturned.'"

Marino's head listed slightly to one side. "Why do you say that?"

"The last man who had your position was beaten to death at a dig site." Tom watched Marino closely. His eyes briefly clouded, then cleared, and his jaw muscle twitched.

"I'll have to dig carefully, then," he said evenly.

Ricky rushed forward, his face flushed. "What are you saying? You saying that Snake—that McCoy—that he wasn't careful? Because he was careful. He had more street smarts and common sense than any man I've ever known. And he was careful."

Tom held up a hand. "Ricky, Ricky. It's okay." He smoothed his tie and motioned to the chair next to Marino's.

"Agent Love," Marino said, leveling his gaze at Ricky, "I certainly didn't mean any disrespect toward Agent McCoy. Please understand. I simply mean to state that I understand the risks involved in working for the FBI. I've had more than a few brushes with danger myself."

A blue vein throbbed in the center of Ricky's forehead as he glared at the man. "Yeah? A few brushes with danger, you say? Well, *Sally*, my friend Snake had more than a brush with danger. He was beaten to a pulp, and nearly every bone in his body was broken when the Japanese Yakuza tortured him. That is, *before* they slashed his throat and left him to bleed out like a stuck hog." He turned his head and glared straight ahead at the wall behind Tom.

Marino spoke softly. "I'm sorry to hear that." He paused, then leaned forward, forcing himself into Ricky's line of vision. "I am not trying to make light of what happened to your friend. But I didn't cause his death, and I won't pay the price for it by being mistreated by you. If I am to work with you and Special Agent Warren, as my orders say I am, then we should do our best to get along. We have to trust each other, and you need to know that I've got your back, even at the risk of losing my own life." Once again he stuck out his hand. "I've got your back, Agent Love. Now do you have mine?"

Ricky huffed, looked at Tom, then turned to face Marino. He stared at the man's hand a moment, then he shook it. Ricky took a deep breath and settled back into his chair, running a hand through his lanky blond hair. "Sorry. Guess I'm just a little raw around the edges."

Marino looked at Ricky, his eyes taking in Ricky's hair, his Hawaiian shirt, his casual pants and shoes. "So am I," he said. "Sorry, I mean, for the loss of your friend. I hear he was a very good man."

Tom smiled, looking down at his hands. "That he was." He sat back and squared his shoulders. "That . . . he . . . was."

Ricky looked at Tom, nodded, then turned to Marino. "And I do have your back. You can trust me. Tom, too."

Tom nodded. "There are some vicious people in the Philippines, and I'm not just referring to the Yakuza." He leveled his gaze at Ricky, then at Marino. "Remember our mission is to get rid of the Commie Huks, who will do whatever it takes to gain control of this country, so we must be on guard at all times. Day and night, understand?"

"Yes, sir. Hoover made that clear when he told me about this position."

Tom cocked an eyebrow. "Hoover? I thought Willoughby chose you for this assignment."

"Willoughby handled the transfer, yes, but Hoover is the one who signed my orders." He hesitated. "I'm sure it was because Willoughby is in Japan with General MacArthur."

Tom looked at Ricky, then back at Marino. "Do you know why they're there?"

"Of course. Military occupation of Japan."

Tom waved his hand. "Good."

Marino cleared his throat. "Right." He nodded to the stack of files on Tom's desk. "You have paperwork for me to fill out, sir?"

Ricky smirked at Tom and tilted his head toward Marino. "You're *asking* for paperwork?"

Marino straightened. "I guess you could say I'm a by-the-book man."

Ricky coughed out a half-laugh. "Good luck with that."

Tom smiled and pulled open his desk drawer, retrieved the file on Marino, and lifted out the first few pages the man would need to complete.

Marino studied Ricky, took in his long hair, his Hawaiian shirt, the way he slouched on the chair. Then he looked at Tom. "I take it you two run a pretty relaxed ship around here."

Tom nodded. "We take care of business, but yes, I guess you could say that. This isn't Quantico."

Salvador Marino's mouth twisted as his eyes again roved Ricky's attire. "You ever think maybe it's too relaxed? Too laid back?"

"What do you mean?" Ricky frowned again, causing deep lines across his forehead.

"What I'm saying is, perhaps if you weren't so laid back, so relaxed . . . perhaps if you were more vigilant, then maybe your friend might . . . well, perhaps he would still be alive today."

Ricky jumped up so fast that his chair fell backward onto the floor. He lunged at Marino, grabbing the man's shirt at the throat.

Tom caught Ricky's arm as he drew back to punch the man. "Stop it! Let him go." He gripped Ricky's arm with both hands, surprised at the strength it took to hold back his punch. "Sit down." He turned to Marino and pointed his finger close to the man's face. "Do *not* antagonize him." He paced angrily across the office and back again, then stopped between the two men, pointing in turn at each as he ranted. "You two have a job to do, and part of that job is to cover my ass. If you're at each other's throats instead of watching my back—and each other's backs—we'll all end up dead." He glared at Ricky. "Just like Snake."

Ricky audibly swallowed.

Tom turned to Marino. "This isn't America. This is the Philippines, and it's a deadly job you have." He pressed his lips together and blew air through his nostrils. "We work damn hard, and sometimes we play hard, too. If you want to push pencils and act like a stuffed suit, then you might want to call your good buddy Hoover back and tell him this isn't the place for you. Around here, we work better if we fit in, not stick out."

Marino stiffened and his upper lip curled. He stood, loosened his tie and yanked the tail of his pressed white shirt from his trousers. He lifted the shirt and the t-shirt beneath it, revealing a hard white belly with three round scars, each the size of a fifty-cent piece. "I'm not afraid of danger, Special Agent Warren. And I'm neither afraid nor opposed to taking a bullet for my partners." He pulled down his shirts, smoothed and tucked them back into his trousers, then readjusted his tie. He leaned forward and locked eyes with Ricky. "I don't care how you dress, and I don't care how long you grow your hair." He then glared at Tom. "And I don't care whether or not you turn in the paperwork I plan to fill out in neat block print with legible cursive signatures. You do your job however you want to do it, but know that I will do mine to the utmost of my God-given ability. By the book." He jutted out his chin and stood straighter. "And I will take a bullet for either of you, understood?"

Chapter 17

January 24, 1949

Hongqiao Airport outside Shanghai, China

RICKY PARKED THE 1947 Cadillac Sedan and jumped out. He climbed into his usual position in the passenger seat of the 1948 Buick Special, and then turned around and winked at Tom in the backseat. "I put the keys under the mat. Whichever one of us gets here first, switch cars."

Sal tromped on the accelerator and they lurched into traffic, heading toward the center of the city.

Ricky leaned over and elbowed Salvatore Marino. "Easy, Sally. This ain't no hotrod."

Ricky looked back at Tom. "We left one car down the street from the restaurant last night while you were visiting with Kung. I got the keys to that car with me."

"Okay. Thanks." Tom turned his attention to the file he'd received from Hoover. As they took a sharp curve, he tilted, nearly dropping the file.

"Everything else set?" Ricky asked.

"Yeah," Tom said, distracted. He set aside his reading and gave his men his attention. "Okay, yes. We're all set. We have two cars near the restaurant. Whoever can get Kung out needs to get back to the big Cadillac, then make like crazy to the airport."

"Why are we doing this in plain view?" Sal asked.

"We have to assume that Kung is being watched, likely by our mysterious Chinese friend or Kang Sheng."

"Whose Kang Sheng?" Sal asked.

"Didn't you read all your background notes, Mr. By-The-Book?" Ricky cast a glare at the driver.

"Hey, they didn't tell me I was coming to China. I studied up on the Philippines."

Tom sighed. "Okay, then. Kang Sheng is the head of Chinese Secret Service—a real bad guy." He leaned forward. "We decided we have a greater chance of being successful extracting him in a crowd of people. If we try to sneak him out from a private setting, we would all end up dead. Kung knows exactly what to do. We will meet him at his favorite restaurant at six."

Ricky turned to face Tom. "What do you know about Kung?"

"Sixty-seven years old. Small, even by Chinese standards."

"What's he look like? How will we recognize him?"

"He's got dark hair—"

"Yeah!" Ricky grunted. "I bet he does. He's Chinese."

Tom ignored him. "He wears it slicked back to cover his bald spot." He leaned forward. "But what sets him apart is that he wears these black-framed eyeglasses with perfectly round lenses."

"Black glasses. Round lenses. Gotcha."

"He's sharp, very sharp. Knows what is going on with the world's economy. He has investments all over the world, including in the US."

Sal glanced at Tom's reflection in the rearview mirror. "Did you ask him about the Federal Reserve Bonds?"

"Of course. He wouldn't tell much, but he did say that Roosevelt sent millions of them over to finance their war with Japan. I got the feeling that, between him, Chiang Kai-shek and T.V. Soong, they have most of them." Tom sucked in his breath. "You know, none of those guys are poor. They could easily manipulate bankers into cooperating with them."

The men grew silent for a few minutes as Tom continued reading the mission file. "Kung has already transferred his accounts out of the country, plus he moved out his cash and gold a while ago." He turned the page. "According to the mission file, his wife, Ai-ling Soong, has already left." Tom closed the file. "Our mission is simple; get Kung out of the country."

Ricky grinned. "So all we have to do is create a disturbance at the restaurant?"

"That should be easy for the two of you, the way you bicker all the time." A grin played across Tom's lips. He'd endured a rough couple of months while his two assistant agents came to terms with each other, but they'd finally settled into an amicable, respectful relationship. "Look, this mission appears more dangerous than I anticipated. Bottom line, H.H. Kung must be on that plane out of here before the Chinese Communists pick him off. We cannot afford to have that happen."

"Are they flying him to America, boss?" asked Ricky.

"No. Hong Kong.

Ricky glanced at Tom. "Is that far enough away? We already know the ChiComs are in Hong Kong, right? We saw that Chinese guy in the gray suit there."

"Of course they are." Tom shrugged. "But that's where Kung wants to go. Ultimately, he wants to end up in the US and live there. I'm betting he has business in Hong Kong before moving on—maybe something else with Izzy. Once he's landed safely in Hong Kong, our mission is over. All we have to do is get him out of Shanghai." He glanced at this watch. Almost six. "Everybody know their assignment? All our escape routes and cars in place?

"Check and double check," Sal said.

"All right, give me about a ten-minute lead in the restaurant." He looked at the back of their heads. "Then you know what to do." Tom placed the file into his briefcase and slid it under the driver's seat. "My briefcase is under your seat, so don't let me forget it. If you have to leave without me, take it to the plane with you."

"What do you mean, without you?" Sal asked.

"I'll get to the plane, some way or another," Tom said.

"I'm not leaving you," Sal caught Tom's eye through the mirror.

"I have my orders, you have yours." Tom raised an eyebrow at Sal's reflected face. "Got it?"

"Got it."

Minutes later, Tom strolled into the restaurant, forcing his arms to swing naturally and his jaw to remain slack. H.H. Kung sat in the back, near the kitchen, just as instructed. Tom side-stepped his way through the crowded restaurant, then casually sat at the table with Kung. He discreetly glanced around to see if they were being watched. Specifically, he wanted to make sure the mysterious Chinese man in the gray suit was nowhere around.

Kung filled Tom's glass from his carafe of wine. They exchanged small talk until the waiter approached and handed out menus. Kung chatted with the waiter for several minutes before either of them opened the menus. The waiter turned and entered the kitchen. Kung and Tom went back to their small talk and sipping wine. Kung refilled each glass.

At the designated minute, Ricky and Sal walked into the restaurant and sat on the opposite side of the large dining room. Each buried his face into his menu.

After a few minutes, the waiter returned to Kung's table. Each man ordered a meal. The waiter bowed, first to Kung, then to Tom, and turned back toward the kitchen.

Tom looked at Kung. In flawless Mandarin, he said, "Mr. Kung, are you ready to go?"

Kung nodded, his eyes squeezed closed.

"Just stay calm. Everything will be fine," Tom said softly. As soon as my men start the disturbance, you go." After about ten minutes, Kung's waiter stepped out of the kitchen and placed meals in front of Kung and Tom. At almost the same time, another waiter came to the table with a carafe of wine, re-filled each glass, then set the bottle in an ice bucket. Using the provided chopsticks, the men ate their meals.

After a minute or two, across the restaurant, Ricky slammed his fist on the table, then jumped up and yelled, "Stop kicking me under the table!"

The restaurant quieted as people turned to check out the commotion.

"I'm not kicking you!" Sal hollered. He looked around sheepishly, then picked up a glass of water, gulped from it, then slammed it back down.

Ricky jumped up from the table. "Now you drank from my water glass! You want that water, then here, take it!" Ricky picked up the glass and threw the water in Sal's face.

As the crowd watched the disturbance, Tom stood, blocking the view of Kung.

Sal stood up nose to nose with Ricky. After a second, he reached for his napkin, wiped his face, then left the table and went into the men's room.

Tom returned to his meal. Kung was no longer across from him. Tom continued eating his meal. He made a point to look around, as though he expected someone to return to the table. Out of the corner of his eye, he thought he saw the Chinese man in the gray suit.

Another movement captured his attention. Across the restaurant, Ricky stood, tossed some money on the table, and strode out of the restaurant.

A tall Chinese man, who had been standing near the door as if waiting for someone, turned and followed Ricky.

Tom's heart lurched. He grabbed the table so as not to run after him.

Another Chinese man, shorter but thickly built, strode toward Tom. Another man—the man in the gray suit!—stepped in pace with the squat man.

Tom jumped up and sprinted toward the kitchen door, knocking over a waiter carrying a tray. Still trying to regain his balance in the confusion of a dozen workers rushing around the too-small kitchen, Tom bounced into one of the kitchen staff. He barely missed a cook carrying a steaming pot. Tom darted, but his balance was lost. He slipped. Before he could regain his footing, cold steel pressed into the back of his head.

Tom eased his hand toward his concealed .38 Special.

"Touch your gun and die," an icy voice said. The henchman jerked Tom's gun from its holster, then pushed Tom toward the back door. Once out of the kitchen, the Chinese henchmen tied Tom's hands with rope, then pulled a dark pillowcase over his head.

Tom was shoved into a car. He closed his eyes and concentrated on breathing—and counting. Should he need to find this place again, knowing how far it was from the restaurant would be helpful. He waited for the car to move. One. Two. Three. What had happened to Kung? Four. Five. Six. To Marino and Love? Seven. Eight. Nine. Had they made it out of there? Ten. Eleven. Twelve. Based upon the sounds and snippets of Chinese he heard, he was the only prisoner. Thirteen. Fourteen. Fifteen. So surely his partners had escaped.

After a short drive—he had only counted to five hundred and six—the car came to a stop. Tom was pulled out of the car and pushed over mixed terrain—some grass, some concrete, perhaps some soil. He stumbled, blindly. Sounds of a door opening and a rush of cool air suggested they had passed through a door and were inside. He was shoved against something—a chair? Pressure on his shoulders forced him to sit—yes, a chair—then someone grabbed his arms and tied them behind him.

A thud sounded near him, followed by a grunt. His heart sank. Someone else had been taken captive. Kung? Ricky? Sal? All the above?

Feet shuffled on the floor to his left. Someone tightened the rope so tightly around his wrists Tom feared it would cut off his circulation. Another rough hand tightened the pillowcase around his neck. He sucked in air with all his might, desperate for any measure of oxygen. His head spun, and he couldn't think straight. He gulped air in deep, heaving breaths, coughing until his throat burned. "Uh ah!" he managed.

No answer. Tom stilled himself in his blindness, tried to steady his breathing, listened for clues. Footsteps across the room ahead of him. Somewhere to his right a clock ticked away excruciatingly slow seconds.

More shuffling, and then loud footsteps faded from the room. Tom listened carefully. Who was the other captive or captives?

Raspy breathing sounded near to his left ear, then a voice spoke harshly. "Do you want your friend to be beaten, or will you help him?"

Chapter 18

January 24, 1949

Somewhere in Shanghai

TWO CHINESE MEN chattered rapidly in a Mandarin dialect. Tom struggled to understand what they were saying. Suddenly, they quieted. "So sorry, doctor. What should we do with the other man?"

Doctor. The man was a doctor. Tom licked his dry lips.

"One last time," said a voice near Tom's ear. "Do you want your friend to be beaten to death? Or will you help him?"

"What do you want from me?" Tom asked, his words thick and raspy.

Someone smacked Tom's face. Numbness covered his cheeks, but was quickly replaced by exploding pain. Tom worked his jaw to test for broken bones.

He heard someone else in the room receive a similar punch. And then another. And another, each one followed by a groan.

"Stop," the other prisoner said quietly. Ricky. It was Ricky.

Tom's heart rate shot up. "What do you want from me?"

The harsh voice was back in his left ear. "Where is Mr. Kung? Your agent took that thief somewhere. Where?"

"I cannot tell you," Tom whispered. His head reeled back with another smack to the face. His cheek and ear burned, and he clenched his teeth.

Ricky screamed out in pain as well. "Don't," he panted, ". . . tell . . . him anything." Another smack sounded across the room, then, another grunt. "They're gonna—" The dull thud of another punch sounded. "Kill us anyway," Ricky finished. Something sizzled, and he again screamed out in pain. Tom's gut wrenched. "What are you doing to him?"

Another hard thwack against the side of head exploded in Tom's ears, causing them to ring. It took more effort to hold up his head this time.

"You will call me *Dr. Wang*." The man speaking into his right ear sucked in a deep breath. "Now tell me, where is the Chinese gold? Where is my family's gold that has been buried in the Philippines?"

They must've busted his head good, because surely he'd not heard correctly. "What?" he whispered. "What did you say?"

That menacing voice of Dr. Wang spoke into his left ear. "You are in the Philippines to discover buried gold for the United States."

Tom forced his brain to work. "No. No. We are there to fight the Philippine Communists. The only gold we saw was being recovered by the Japanese Yakuza. The same Yakuza who'd killed our partner, Snake."

Another agonizing scream came from Ricky

The heavy breath sounded again by his ear, and then the voice. "My men are applying pressure to his various wounds. To stop the bleed, do you understand?"

Tom struggled against the ropes cutting into his wrists. He had to save Ricky. He hadn't been able to save Snake, but he could save Ricky. "Please stop hurting him! I cannot tell you anything about Kung. Once Kung got to the airport, the plane was ready to go and leave immediately."

"So he is on a plane." Dr. Wang breathed into his ear, so closely now that he could feel and smell his foul breath. "A plane to where?"

Tom strained to orient himself, moving his head around under the dark pillowcase. A punch he didn't hear coming hit his head so hard he saw stars.

The harsh voice was back in his left ear. "Agent Warren, I am holding myself back from killing the both of you right now. It is even more difficult to control my men. Do you understand me? If my men did not respect me, both of you would be dead, and your bodies would already be cold."

Tom nodded, struggling to stay conscious in the darkness. Again, he heard Ricky scream out in agony.

Footsteps faded out of the room, then all went quiet.

⇥● ●⇤

Tom struggled to stay awake. His head leaned forward, and if it weren't for the ropes holding him, he'd fall headlong. But he had to stay awake. "Ricky?" he whispered.

There was no answer.

Tom wanted to try again, but the effort was too much. *Just stay awake. Don't give in.* He tried to think of how many words rhymed with "light." Bright. Kite. Might. Fight. But even the mind games he was so good at playing were failing him. "Ricky." He barely breathed the words.

A door squeaked open and footsteps grew closer. Tom's stomach churned. He hoped they'd kill them fast and omit the torture, but that wasn't likely.

Someone pinched the back of his neck, over and over. Then pillowcase was ripped off his head. Tom blinked against the glaring lights. And then a thought hit him. They were going to make him watch as they tortured Ricky. Vomit climbed his esophagus. He looked around the room the best he could. Ricky was about twenty feet from him, in a similar wooden chair, his head covered and his hands tied. From the way he was slumped forward, it was obvious he was unconscious. That voice, that evil voice, was back in his ear. "Agent Warren, I am going to save your life and your friend's life, but this will be the last time. Do you understand me?"

Before Tom could react to this news, a hard blow hit the back of his head, knocking both him and the chair he was tied to over. Blackness teased his peripheral vision, threatening to take his consciousness. If he were to succumb to the darkness, he and Ricky would surely die.

One of the large henchmen lunged for Tom. But instead of hitting him or kicking him, he grabbed him, chair and all, and set him upright.

And that voice, that evil voice, was back in his left ear. "Agent Warren, Kang Sheng wanted me to give you a message for Mr. J. Edgar Hoover. We want Mr. Kung and all of his assets returned to Chairman Mao. Do you understand me?"

Tom sucked in a breath of stale air. They weren't going to kill him. Ricky was already unconscious, so they wouldn't have any joy in beating on him. "May I ask a question, doctor?"

The henchman on Tom's left raised his hand to strike, but Dr. Wang lifted a finger and stayed the man's hand. "Ask, but do not expect an answer." He turned his back to Tom and walked toward the doorway, where he stood motionless.

"Where are the stolen US printing press and plates?"

Wang turned his head to look at Tom, clearly surprised, then turned again to face the window. "I do not know. Nor do I care." He clasped his small hands behind his back. "The Nationalists probably have them." His shoulders shrugged almost imperceptibly. "The Communists have no need for them." Dr. Wang clenched his fists, paced across the room and back, then stopped in front of Tom. He closed his eyes and exhaled a long, even breath through his nose, flaring his nostrils. When he opened his eyes, his icy, calm façade had returned. He kept his eyes on Tom, but spoke to his henchmen. "Take them to Larry Wu-tai Chin."

The henchman swung around. "Wu-tai Chin?"

"Yes. At the US Consulate."

The henchman chuckled. "Good thinking, sir. Good thinking."

Chapter 19

January 25, 1949
Hong Kong, China

TOM INTERMITTENTLY GLARED at people or looked away to repel and avert stares from the patrons in the hotel lobby where he and his men still had reserved rooms. Of course he looked horrible. His hands found their way to his face, and he gingerly fingered the lumpy cheekbones, the swollen nose, the cut lips. He avoided the mirror behind the lobby desk. What was the use? He could hardly see through the slits of his puffy eyes. Tom was just grateful that the consulate in Shanghai had cleaned them up, put him and Ricky on a plane back to Hong Kong where they could meet up with Sal.

Keeping his face toward the wall, Tom sidled toward the elevator, and he kept his chin tucked as he awaited its arrival from an upper floor. After what seemed like an hour, the elevator finally thumped to its landing, and the door opened. A woman adjusting her gloves nearly bumped into him, and when she looked up to apologize, she gasped in shock.

The crowd parted around him, giving him wider berth than required. Others filtered into the car, and when Tom stepped in, a white-haired woman wearing a hat overflowing with flowers raised her eyebrows, opened her mouth in surprise and quickly stepped out. She hustled in short, quick steps away from the elevator, looking back over her shoulder as if fearing Tom might follow her. Others in the elevator huddled against the wall away from Tom, and he turned with his back toward them, facing the still-open doors. As he watched the older woman scurry away, the doors slowly began to close. As they did, he saw his tormentor—Dr. Wang—talking to someone twice his size—a Caucasian—in the far corner of the lobby. *How had Wang gotten there?* And why? Was he looking for Tom?

Dr. Wang pulled his hand out from his gray suit jacket and produced a fat, white envelope. As the elevator doors finally met, Tom recognized the big man talking with Dr. Wang. It was the priest!

Tom's mouth went dry. What was Father Diaz doing in Hong Kong? And why was he taking money—it had to be money, didn't it?—why was he taking money from Dr. Wang? Had Wang paid the priest to get to H.H. Kung? Had he bought information? Or was Wang paying him to keep an eye on Tom back in the Philippines? It could not be a coincidence that Dr. Wang and the priest were meeting in the very hotel in which Tom and his men had rooms.

A thought dawned on him then, one that chilled him. What if Wang was there because of Izzy? If the man knew she'd tried to do business with H.H. Kung, he might try to hurt her.

The elevator lurched to a stop, and people exited on either side of Tom. He stood rooted as the doors closed again, and too late, he realized he'd missed his floor. His head reeled. As the elevator moved upward, Tom punched the button for the floor they'd just departed.

"Hey, buddy," said a gravelly voice from behind Tom, "we just left that floor."

Tom turned and scowled, his mangled face speaking without words. The man averted his gaze and shrank against the wall.

Tom ran through at least a dozen scenarios involving Wang and Father Diaz as the elevator rose to the upper floors, then finally descended back to his level. He stepped out, automatically reaching for the gun he no longer had, and looked up and down the garishly carpeted hallway. He was alone. Tom walked cautiously toward his room, thankful that Ricky, Sal and he hadn't checked out. He realized then that he didn't have a key to his room. His shoulders sank and he heaved a deep sigh. No way he could go back to the lobby to ask the concierge for another key to his room, not with Dr. Wang and Father Diaz there. Wang had made it perfectly clear that he'd kill him if he ever saw him again. Tom again touched his stinging split lip. He believed the man.

He read the numbers on the hotel doors, trying to remember which was Ricky's and which was Sal's. Four-oh-seven. Seven was Sal's lucky number. He walked past his own room and knocked on the door to four-eleven. "Be here, Ricky, c'mon, be here," Tom whispered.

When he heard rustling in the room, Tom cocked his elbow in the air and stepped to the side of the door. If Dr. Wang knew they were staying in the hotel, he could have set a trap. His henchmen could be in the room, going through Ricky's things.

The door swung open, but no one appeared. Tom flattened against the wall. He wished he had a gun, a knife, a stick, anything. His fist would have to do. He tightened it, ready to come down on the first thing appearing in the doorway. Which was a gun. Tom's right fist slammed down on the top of the revolver. At the same time, he swung around, his left fist coming up within an inch of the gun owner's face.

"Boss?"

It was Ricky. Just Ricky. Relief washed over Tom.

"What the hell was that?" Ricky demanded. "You knock on my door and then accost me?"

"You greeted me with a gun!"

Ricky's swollen and bruised face erupted into a grin. "Get in here." He slid the pistol into his waistband. "Damn, you're a sight for sore eyes," he said, closing the door behind them.

Tom's lip felt too tight as he smiled. "Your eyes are sore, too?"

Ricky grunted, walked across the room, filled a glass with water and soaked a washcloth, then offered both to Tom.

Tom gulped the water, sat down the glass and winced as he dabbed carefully at his aching face.

"Sally and Kung made it?" Ricky asked.

"Yes, I just checked with authorities to see how Kung was doing. And Sal is here, in his room." Tom held up the empty water glass. "Got anything any stronger?"

"Ordered it as soon as I got here." Ricky reached behind his nightstand and held up a bottle of liquor. "It ain't moonshine, but it'll have to do." He offered a cheerless smile, and instead of filling the glass, he handed the half-full bottle to Tom.

Tom twisted off the lid and took several swallows of the bitter, searing liquid, cringing from the burn. Then he held the washcloth to the bottle opening and saturated one corner with the liquor. He held his breath and dabbed the alcohol onto his torn lip, unabashedly letting tears seep from his eyes.

Ricky winced as he watched. "That thing needs stitches."

Tom sniffed as his nose began to run. "You qualified?"

"Me? I don't think so."

"Well, you're the only one who can do it. We can't go anywhere for a while." He looked around as though making sure no one else was in the room, then lowered his voice. "I just saw Dr. Wang downstairs."

Ricky's eyebrows shot skyward. "What! You're kidding me. How did he— does he know we're here?" He hustled to the door, slid the metal peephole cover to one side and peered out.

"I don't think so. I'm pretty sure he's here for other reasons."

"What other reasons?"

Tom delicately probed his cut lip with the tip of his tongue. "I saw him hand a fat envelope to Father Diaz in the lobby."

"Fath—what in the world? What is the priest doing here?"

Tom shrugged, threw back another swig of liquor and dabbed again at his lip with the alcohol-saturated cloth. This time it didn't hurt as much.

Ricky's squinted through swollen eyelids. "You okay? You sure you don't have a concussion or something?"

Tom chuckled. "I'm pretty sure I wasn't seeing things. Although it does sound kinda farfetched."

"Ricky grabbed the bottle from Tom and threw back a long swallow. "Was he dressed as a priest?"

"No. He was wearing that gaudy cross of his, though. Other than that, he could've been anyone."

Ricky let out a low whistle and ran a hand through his freshly washed blond hair. "What do you think was in the envelope?"

"Money. It was the right size for a stack of greenbacks."

"American money?"

"Does it matter?" Tom took possession of the bottle again and gulped another long swig.

Ricky took the bottle from Tom's hand. "You might want to take it easy on that. After the twenty-four hours we've had, we need to stay as alert as we can—especially with Dr. Wang in the building."

"I think we're okay, as long as we lay low for a few hours."

Ricky studied Tom for a minute. "Get some sleep, then. I'll stand guard." He walked to each of the large windows and pulled the curtains shut, dimming the room considerably. He carried an armchair and placed in front of the door, then sank heavily onto it. "Just in case I nod," he said. "You sleep here instead of going to your room."

"No choice in the matter. The lackeys took my keys."

"Mine, too, but the maid let me in." He smiled a tight, crooked smile. "Take my bed. We'll log a couple of hours of zzzs, get showers, and then leave after dark."

"Think I should call Izzy?" Tom slurred around the heiress's name.

Ricky's face went lax. "Why would you do that?"

"What if Wang is here for her? What if he tries to hurt her?"

Ricky shook his head. "She's got plenty of security at her beck and call. Rest first. Then we'll go see her face-to-face. If you bring up Dr. Wang's name, you need to see her reaction first-hand."

Tom wrinkled his forehead. "What do you mean?"

"We hardly know this woman. For all we know, she could be in cahoots with Wang. Or the priest. Or both."

Tom's mind clamped shut. He couldn't process anything else right now. "I need to lie down. We'll talk about this when I wake up."

⊷═◉ ◉═⊷

Tom opened his eyes in the unfamiliar room. Where was he? He rose on one elbow, tried to focus on his surroundings. Ricky's room.

Slowly he stood, walked over and sank onto a padded armchair, leaned back his head and closed his eyes. "How long did we sleep?"

"Me? About six hours. You logged fourteen."

"Fourteen!" Tom bolted upright. "Why didn't you wake me?" He groaned as he leaned over and pushed aside the curtain, revealing early evening dusk.

Ricky cocked his head. "Like you'd have been good for anything, in the shape you were in. Besides, you downed plenty of liquor before you wiped out. Figured if you didn't get enough sleep after that noggin-pounding you took, you might end up with another migraine."

Tom shook his head. He looked around Ricky's hotel room. No evidence existed that either of them had stayed there. The glasses they'd drank from the night before were no longer in sight, and when he looked toward the small bathroom, he saw all clean towels hanging evenly on the rack. "Where is Sal? Housekeeping been here?"

"Sal has been keeping watch over us. Can't let anyone in here, with Dr. Wang and the so-called priest lurking around." He jutted his chin. "I cleaned the room myself. In case we have to leave in a hurry. Didn't want any trace of us."

"No trace of us," Tom muttered, massaging his still-aching jaw. Maybe that wasn't the best way to say it. "Maybe Sal can get us some coffee."

Ricky left the room. Ten minutes later, Sal returned with bitter black coffee and Tom's room key. Tom added a splash of the rock-gut liquor to his cup, and downed it while it still steamed. He stood and headed toward the door, picking up the key. "I'm going next door to shower. After I get cleaned up, we'll order dinner and another bottle of whatever that stuff is we've been drinking, then we'll send a message to Izzy."

Ricky nodded as Tom ambled across the floor like an old man. "Hey, boss?"

"Yeah?"

"Don't make a mess over there. I'm not your maid."

Tom provided an obscene gesture for Ricky's amusement, then continued on his way.

Chapter 20

SANTA ROMANA'S HEAD nodded and his eyelids drooped. He jerked himself awake. The two cups of coffee he'd had at the airport wore off some time ago. He pulled off the road—again—and stepped out of the car. He breathed in the fresh night air and looked up at the brilliant starlit night. *Thank you, Lord, for your splendid glory.*

His day in Hong Kong had been long, eventful and very successful. Well, for the most part. He'd set up new bank accounts to handle both his own gold and some for the CIA. He had opened a walk-in vault at one of the banks to handle some of his more prized discoveries. All had gone without a hitch, except. . . .

Except that meeting with Lieu Xu-Jiang, his former bank officer from the Bank of Communication. It had not been what one would call successful. Santa Romana had learned Lieu Xu-Jiang was a Chinese agent, which was why he'd moved his accounts from the Chinese bank to the one in Hong Kong. But Xu-Jiang—also known as *Dr. Wang*—had relentlessly pressed him to identify where the Chinese gold was buried in the Philippines. Santa Romana continued to lead him on, particularly since Xu-Jiang paid him cash almost every time they met. *Fat chance I will ever help those communists. I will use them, I will bait them, but I will never show them, give them, sell them any of this gold. I will not let either of those maniacs, Xu-Jiang nor Mao, gain any power.*

Santa Romana filled his lungs with one more serving of moist Filipino air, then returned to his car and continued driving toward his church. Maybe the meeting with Xi-Jiang was successful. It certainly has been so financially. *Oh, sweet Jesus, let me get home before these tired eyes close.* He turned on the radio and fidgeted with the tuner, but there was nothing but static at this hour. The ninety-minute drive from the airport in Manila seemed to take forever.

Finally, as he rounded the last turn, the faint outline of the white steeple glowed in the moonlight. With joy, he pulled into the driveway behind the church. Once out of the car, he let out a breath of air. Santa Romana pulled out his key and stuck it in the door lock. Instead of smoothly sliding in as it normally did, it jammed. He took it out and made sure he had the right key. There was no doubt—the brass key was the largest on his chain, always standing out. He tried again. Still it wouldn't go. Now keenly awake, he walked back over to his car and removed the flashlight and his handgun out of the glove box. He shined the light on the door lock. Yes, it had been tampered with. With a grimace, he forced the key into the lock. It went in, but he had to jiggle it to finally get it to turn and release the lock.

Santa Romana pushed open the door, then quietly and methodically he shined the flashlight around the office. No one was there. He glided from one side of the office to the other, not making a sound, then entered the sanctuary and again flashed his light around the much larger room. Nothing. The yellowish beam of his flashlight illuminated the elaborately carved crucifix. It was still there, unmarred. He returned to his office and flipped on the overhead light.

Immediately, his eyed locked on his desk. Whenever he was out, he left everything on his desk the exact same way—the ball point pen in the groove on the right-hand side of the old wooden desk, his bible in the center with ground palm leaves sprinkled over it, and the notepad on the left, waiting for words of wisdom or a quick note. But the bible wasn't angled the way he always left it, slightly askew, and the ground palm leaves were disturbed. The pen was still in place, and the notepad appeared intact.

Why would someone enter his church office? What would they be looking for in a holy place? He went to the hidden trap door that led to his hideout. The small piece of matchbook cover was still in place, indicating it had not likely been opened. He lifted up the loose floorboards and descended under the church. Everything appeared untouched. Whoever had been there had not discovered his secret.

Swiftly, he ascended the steps and went to examine the cabinet that held the communion chalice and plate. His journal was still there on top, right where he'd left it. But the scrap of paper left in it lay on the floor. His journal had been opened. He picked it up and rifled through the pages. Nothing missing. And, of course, it contained nothing important—nothing that would implicate him. Then he opened the ambry containing the gold chalice and matching ciborium used for communion. They were missing! Pope Pius had not only handed him those items directly, he had blessed them.

Panic clenched his gut. He slid the bottom draw open and looked under the sacramental cloths. It was missing. The sapphire rosary, the second one, the one inscribed with the Greek letter *omega*.

Sweet Mary, Mother of Jesus, please let there be a mistake. Please don't let the rosary be taken. One by one, he took out the cloths and set them on the altar, making sure the rosary hadn't slipped into a fold or fallen between the linens. Each time he examined a cloth, his heart sank deeper. It was gone. He knew it in his gut. It was gone.

He laid the last cloth on the altar, then ran his hand over the drawer. Empty. Not even a dust bunny. He looked to the left and to the right. On the floor. But it was gone.

Father Diaz fell to the floor, draping his large shoulders over the open drawer. The value of that rosary was not in the sapphires and diamonds set in its gold. He closed his eyes tight. Pope Pius had personally called upon him for a special mission. It was January, 1938, and the Pope was only too aware that the Nazis would soon loot the Vatican and take all its gold and treasure. Because of Father Diaz's loyal service and dedication, the Pope chose him to accompany the Vatican Guard in transporting the Vatican gold to the one place that seemed far from the clutches of Hitler—the Philippines. As a thank you, Pope Pius presented Father Diaz with two identical rosaries crafted from gold and containing diamonds and star sapphires. The Pope blessed the rosaries before handing them to Father Diaz. "God bless you for your service, and may these rosaries serve as physical amulets of the power and protection of our Lord Jesus Christ."

Unfortunately, the gold fell into the hands of the Japanese, as did the gold belonging to the Chinese and many of the other allied nations—a misdeed Father Diaz dedicated the remainder of his life to correcting by whatever means he could. The rosaries were a reminder of the Pope's faith in him. To the "Alpha" and "Omega" originally inscribed on them, he added his own inscriptions—passcodes to the recaptured gold—so that someday, he could re-store to the Vatican what was rightfully its.

In July, 1943, he had given one of the rosaries to the distraught widow of a close friend and comrade. She had no clue the importance of what she held, although the power of the rosaries were not in one alone, but in the two of them held side-by-side.

And now the second rosary was gone, and he had not a clue as to where it could be.

Chapter 21

TOM PADDED BAREFOOT out of the steamy bathroom wearing black slacks and an unbuttoned white shirt. He toweled his hair and headed toward the partially filled open suitcase he'd laid on the bed, following Ricky's good advice to be ready to leave.

A knock sounded at the door. Ricky had been nursing an upset stomach and said he was turning in early, so he wouldn't be knocking. Tom dropped the socks back into the suitcase and picked up his pistol, holding it at the small of his back, beneath his shirttail.

Spying through the peephole, he was surprised to see Izzy. He started to put the gun down, but on second thought, he tucked it into his waistband and buttoned a couple of lower buttons on his shirt to hide it. "Coming," he called, smoothing back his hair.

He opened the door and Izzy walked in, wearing a gleaming mink coat that nearly skimmed the floor. She stared at his battered face, then eyed him up and down, her gaze unabashedly lingering on his chest.

She reached out, allowing her fingers to trace ever so softly down his bruised cheek. Then she took a step backward and looked up at him through large, long-lashed eyes. "Mr. Kung asked me to convey to you his gratitude for getting him out of the country."

Tom opened his mouth to speak, but she held a finger close to his mouth, though didn't touch him. He inhaled her scent. Musky sweetness swirled into his consciousness, taking with it all the oxygen in the room.

She giggled through glossy red lips, then slowly trailed her fingers down the collar of her mink coat and suggestively slid them inside the neckline. She gave a violent pull with her hands, flinging the coat open, then let it slide down her arms to the floor, like melting chocolate.

She stood before him, a red-haired goddess standing in a puddle of fur, perfectly naked.

Chapter 22

Manila, Philippines
January 30, 1949

IT WAS TOM'S first day back in his office, and he stood rifling through a stack of mail. He noticed a large manila envelope, picked it up and opened it. It was a letter from Judy. It still smelled of her.

> *Thomas,*
>
> *I hope this letter finds you well.*
>
> *I am writing to let you know I've met someone quite wonderful. His name is William Carter, and we are to be married in two weeks.*
>
> *Please be happy for me. I simply could not wait any longer for you, and you and I both know you're not ready to settle down and raise a family.*
>
> *I wish the best for you.*
>
> *Fondly,*
>
> *Judy*

Tom sat heavily at his desk and stared at the plain stationary as a minute ticked past. Though the handwriting was as familiar to him as his own, the tone remained foreign. Unlike her previous letters, there were no admissions of love, no pleas for him to return soon to her arms. He stared at the closing and read it aloud to the empty room. "Fondly, Judy." *Fondly.* This was what he'd become—someone she was fond of. His eyes caressed the loops and curves he found so familiar. He held the single sheet of paper, folded in thirds. Her words were already inscribed on his brain and would likely remain there until the day he died—one of the drawbacks of his unusual memory. He touched the words she had written, then held the paper to his nose and sniffed.

He tucked the letter back into the envelope and looked again at the postmark. It was a month old. She was already married.

⊶⊷

Ferdinand Marcos boarded a borrowed yacht in Manila Bay and headed out to sea. About ten miles out, another yacht sat still in the open sea. On the bow of that ship was his friend and business partner, Japanese-American Fukimatsu Minoru. Marcos pulled his boat even with Minoru's and boarded the exotic ship.

The two men bowed to each other, then wordlessly walked toward the stern and ducked below deck. They entered the large stateroom and sat at a table that displayed a gold chalice, a gold plate and a sapphire rosary. Minoru handed Marcos a glass of fine brandy, and they touched glasses.

Minoru pointed with his lips. "This is *all* my friends were able to find in the priest's church. My senses tell me there is more."

Marcos looked at the items with great disappointment. "No ledger? Nothing of importance?"

Minoru shook his head. "They thoroughly searched the church. Nothing. I told them not to come back empty-handed, so they took these items."

Marcos stood, walked over and looked out one of the stateroom windows. After a minute, he turned. "Why did they have to take the communion chalice and plate?"

Minoru stared at his friend, then said, "There is more, somewhere. The journal kept behind his desk states these items were given to him by the Pope. The sapphire rosary was blessed by Pope Pius."

Marcos pressed his lips tightly together and stared at Minoru. "I need to know more about this man. I am in business with him, and I only know things about him that he wants me to know. Why do the Huks trust him? Why are they scared of him? Is he Santa Romana or Father Diaz? Or someone else? I need to control him, and right now, he controls me." Marcos pushed away from the table. "I need some dirt."

He scooped up the sapphire rosary and examined it closely. Star sapphires—except for one gold bead linking to the chain that ended with the cross.

"Get me more." He stuck the rosary in his pocket and exited the stateroom.

Chapter 23

Manila, Philippines
April 27, 1949

Tom took a long drag from his cigarette, dropped the butt on the ground and snubbed it out with his shiny black shoes. He bent down, picked it up and tossed it into the metal barrel that served as a trash can.

"You're the only man in the Philippines who does that." Sal waved a hand toward the edge of the sidewalk, littered with at least a dozen cigarette butts. "How do you even know which one is yours?"

Ricky chuckled.

"I prefer to think of it as the difference between the civilized and the uncivilized," Tom said. "Besides, it's good practice when you're on surveillance to not leave any evidence." He straightened his collar and peered up and down the street, scanning the crowd for any sign of Candy Man. "Where is he, anyway?" He looked at the sky, where the sun now rose directly overhead, then checked his watch. "He should've been here ten minutes ago."

Sal kicked at trash blowing along the sidewalk. "Maybe he's getting a juicy tidbit from Luis Taruc."

"I still have a hard time trusting him," Ricky said.

Sal drew his head back and studied Ricky. "He's been very careful about where he gets his information, since your buddy got killed on the mountain."

Ricky pressed his lips together, but eventually nodded. "He damn well should."

"I have to admit," Tom said, "we're closing in on the Commies, and we wouldn't be nearly as far along if it wasn't for that dirt bag. Willoughby was right; the man sings like a canary when you butter his palm."

Ricky nodded toward the far end of the street. "Well, Candy Man can't be talking with Taruc, because Taruc is right down there."

Tom turned casually and glanced around in both directions.

Sal stepped forward to look. "Who's that with him? I can't see his face."

"That's William Pomeroy," Ricky said.

Tom let out a soft whistle. "Pomeroy and Taruc. I knew from a file that Hoover sent over that Pomeroy was a full blown commie, but what is Pomeroy doing with Taruc?"

Ricky said, "Word is Pomeroy came back to the Philippines and is writing Taruc's memoirs."

Tom stroked his chin. "It's making sense now. Pomeroy just became our top priority. We put a tail on him, *immediately*." He smoothed back his hair and stared at the sky as he rearranged pieces of the puzzle in his mind. "I'll bet I know why Dr. Wang has been visiting the Philippines, and it's not all about the gold."

Sal looked sharply at Tom. "What do you mean?"

Three Filipinos wearing white barong tagalongs ran side-by-side down the sidewalk, the men on each end spinning loud, clacking noisemakers. "We won! We won!" shouted the one in the center. Behind them, the crowd grew and surged as more revelers joined the ruckus.

"What in the—" Tom turned as a Filipina wearing flowers in her hair waved a flag across his face as she ran past.

A man behind her stepped between Tom and Sal, then ripped a poster off a brick wall between storefronts. *Marcos for CONGRESS!* the poster read. The man held it up, waving it over his head. "We won! God bless Ferdinand Marcos!" He grinned, revealing a missing front tooth. "We won! We won!"

Sal stared at Tom. "Marcos won the election?" He shook his hand. "My friend, we were in Hong Kong way too long."

"Hello, my friend," Candy Man said in Tagalog and clapped Ricky on the back.

"Where have you been?" Tom asked. "You're late."

"Yes, yes, look at the crowd." Candy Man waved his hands in the air. "The streets around Malacañang Palace are impassible, and I had a terrible time getting here."

Another trio of men jogged past, one of them bumping Ricky, knocking him off-balance into Tom. Tom caught him by the arms. "Whoa, nelly."

Ricky shook his hair from his eyes and frowned. "Let's get out of here. Too much going on to spot trouble before it gets here. "

The four men headed down the street. As they reached the corner of an alley, Candy Man nodded toward a bar. "In here," he said as the alley filled with street vendors.

Tom snorted. The Filipinos always seemed ready to celebrate a political victory—even a perceived one—and were just as ready with their wares to make a profit from it.

The bar smelled of spicy sausage and cigarette smoke, and Tom wrinkled his nose. It took a moment for his eyes to adjust to the dim room. He looked around, realized the only light in the place was what struggled to penetrate the dingy windows. Leave it to Candy Man to pick a classy joint.

Candy Man led them to an even darker corner near the back of the nearly empty place. Tom sat on the wooden bench next to Ricky, and big Sal slid onto the bench beside of Candy Man, practically pinning the man against the wall.

Tom took a deep breath. He felt the greasy, smoky air permeate his lungs, felt his throat clog. He cleared his throat and stared at Candy Man. "What do you have for us?"

The dark-haired man turned his palms upward, grinned and motioned to the bar for wait service. "What's the rush, my friend? Today is a day of celebration. Let's have a drink."

The bartender-turned-waiter stepped to their table, his barong tagalong dingy gray in the dim light. Tom ordered a bottle of whiskey and four glasses, then clasped his hands together on the table and leaned forward, his face serious. "Ricky said you have news for me." He set his jaw. "Let's hear it."

Candy Man held up his hands. "Okay, sure, sure. You take the fun out of good news, Mister Tom." His eyes glittered. "I have an appointment arranged for you tonight." He paused, making Tom wait for the rest.

Tom gritted his teeth. The place reeked, the whiskey would likely be watered down, and he'd already had enough of this cheesy little man. Unbidden, an image of Isabella Scarborough rose to his mind, her froth of red curls, her tiny, pouty lips, her ivory skin. Right now, she was probably enrobed in peach satin while lounging in her luxurious penthouse, while he sat here amid the stink of a greasy bar.

"—First Lady Aurora Quezon!" Candy Man smacked the table, bringing Tom back to the present. "See? I told you I would come through for you." Candy Man beamed like a proud child.

Tom glanced at Ricky and Sal, then back at Candy Man. He'd missed everything. "Say again?"

"The First Lady. She wants to meet with you. Tonight!" Candy Man held up his glass for a toast. Ricky and Sal clinked theirs against his, and Tom slowly lifted his to the occasion.

"You say . . . the late President Manuel Quezon's wife . . . she wants to meet with me? Tonight?" Tom took a small sip. "Why?"

Candy Man's happy face wilted. "You want to ask questions, yes? You want to know about the gold? Who better to answer than First Lady Aurora Quezon?" He leaned forward conspiratorially. "You can believe whatever she says. She is a saint. A real saint. Do you know that Pope Pius XII gave her the *Pro Ecclessia et Pontifice Cross*? She will tell you the truth. Whatever you ask her." Candy Man sat back, squaring his shoulders and thrusting out his chest.

Tom scowled. It sounded like a trap. He pierced Candy Man with his eyes and spoke in staccato words, enunciating carefully. "Why—does—she—want—to—meet—with—me?"

Candy Man's mouth opened, and he looked incredulous. "You are FBI! First Lady Quezon loves Americans." He shook his head, shrugged and turned up his palms. "Your country cared for her husband. President Manuel Quezon died in New York. She believes you are her people, just like we are her people." His lower lip protruded and his voice took on a whine. "Your country helped her start the Red Cross here, after all. Maybe she feels gratitude to your people." He sat quietly for a moment, then he leaned forward and tapped the table. "Did you know some university in America gave her a doctor's degree? See! She is an American doctor! That is probably why." He sat back with a satisfied grin, as if that explained everything.

Tom looked around the dingy room. The bartender stood with his back to the men, wiping glasses with a grubby towel. A few customers gathered at the front, rowdy and drunk, yelling in a dialect Tom didn't recognize. He picked up his glass, swirled the dark amber liquid, and stared into it as if looking for answers. It wasn't every day he met a former First Lady. And Candy Man was probably right about her being honest. Since he'd arrived in the Philippines four years ago, he'd heard of the woman's kindnesses and charitable acts. She'd even refused the pension awarded her as wife of the late president, saying the war widows deserved the money more than she did.

He downed a swig of the liquor, surprised it tasted as good as it did. He licked his lips, then looked at Candy Man. "What time?"

Chapter 24

TOM SMOOTHED HIS tie and smiled at the lovely, white-haired woman who daintily sipped from her teacup.

"My husband also favored pinstripe suits," former First Lady Aurora Quezon said. "You make a handsome young man."

Tom's smile turned to a grin. *Young man.* No wonder everyone loved this portly lady. Instead of the stuffy meeting with a former president's wife he'd prepared for, he found himself wanting to curl his feet beneath him, rest his chin in his hand and ask her to tell him a story. She felt like the kind of mother—or perhaps grandmother—he'd always wanted.

"So you have recently returned from Hong Kong? A lovely, lovely city, though I'm sure it's changed quite a bit since I was last there." Her gaze took in the room around her, then wistfully settled on a photo of her and President Manual Quezon taken during his inauguration. "The President and I were married in Hong Kong." The corners of her eyes pleasantly crinkled when she smiled. "Baby, our daughter, was born just over a year later. Oh, I know, one shouldn't call a grown woman *Baby*—*Maria* is her name—but we called her our baby for so long that it stuck." Her eyes twinkled. "Did you know she is here?" The woman nodded as she spoke. "Yes, she's a student, you know, at University of Santo Tomas. She studies law. Perhaps she will follow in her father's footsteps." Mrs. Quezon beamed a smile at Tom, then seemed to realize he hadn't spoken in a while. She put a hand to her lips, and her cheeks colored. "Forgive me. I am an old lady who talks too much."

"Nonsense!" Tom could spend hours watching the way her eyes sparkled and her hands fluttered as she spoke. She enthralled him. "Please continue."

She waved away his kindness. "You came to speak with me." She lifted the teapot from the table between them.

The young housekeeper stepped forward to assist, but Mrs. Quezon motioned for her to leave them alone. The woman stepped just outside of the room, alert should she be needed.

"How may I help you, Agent Warren?"

Tom held out his cup and saucer as the first lady poured with a steady hand. "Please, I would be honored if you would call me Tom."

"The honor is mine, Tom." She gently set the teapot back on the tray and offered sugar cubes to Tom.

He took one, stirred it into his tea, and placed his spoon on the edge of his saucer. He lifted his cup and sat back on his chair, but didn't sip. Not yet. He didn't want to offend this kind woman, but he needed answers. "I fear my questions might insult your graciousness, First Lady. However, I come on behalf of my government." He bowed his head in acquiescence. "And I'm afraid I must ask anyway."

She offered a slight shrug. "I am too old to be easily insulted." She peered intently at Tom. "Besides, I have a question of my own to ask of you."

Tom nodded, relieved. "Please, go ahead."

She smiled. "You are my guest. Speak first."

Tom sucked in a long, slow breath. Why did he feel nervous? He looked at the elegantly rotund woman, and she leaned forward, encouraging him with a nod. He quietly cleared his throat. "Mr. Hoover sent me here to help the Filipino government rid the country of the communist guerilla movement, which has evolved into the Hukbalahap movement. I think there is more to this situation than the official government story reveals. What can you tell me about your husband's efforts to put them down?

Mrs. Quezon's plump face crinkled. "I thought that was your friend's job to explain this to you. Your friend, the one you call Candy Man." She paused, sizing Tom up. "You know his family is one of the old, wealthy families. He has long been a member of the Hukbalahaps. Did you know that, Tom?"

Tom said, "No, ma'am, I didn't. What else can you tell me about the Huks?"

"You know about Luis Taruc, yes?"

"Yes. And his right-hand man, Guillermo Capadocia."

"Well, you better watch out for Emeterio Anthonyban and Jose Alejandrino. There are many others, they all have their own little—oh, what shall I say—*kingdoms* they ruled." She paused to take a delicate sip of tea. "You know MacArthur arrested Taruc and Alejandrino two separate times. He must have thought they were important."

"Yes, I am aware, but there was no official record of the interrogations."

"That's funny; my husband said the same thing. He tried to get information on the interrogation and got stonewalled." She set down her teacup. "Do you have any other questions for me?"

"What do you know about any US printing presses and US currency plates?"

Her eyes widened, but she cleared her throat, then picked up her teacup and continued. "I don't know what you're talking about. We didn't have anything to do with anything like that."

Tom wondered if he should continue asking questions, or call it a night. What did he have to lose? "Do you know anything about the treasures and gold the Japanese stole from the Chinese? It is reported to be buried here in the Philippines."

First Lady Quezon chuckled, her powdered cheeks quivering. "Oh, since the middle of the war, we knew the Japanese were doing something on the islands, but we were afraid to go around. Seemed anyone who did, never came back." She shook her head and her face darkened. "I have no doubt the Japanese robbed the Chinese. It was a terrible, terrible tragedy, the atrocities that happened over there." She stared into her teacup, reflecting. Then she looked at Tom, her eyes clear. "Any treasures they captured sank in the ocean. A fitting burial at sea."

"You don't believe Yamashita commanded slaves to bury the stolen war loot in tunnels dug into the mountains outside of Manila?"

"Oh, I don't know!" First Lady Quezon's face retained its pleasant appearance. "I really do not know. Treasure seekers have been digging in those mountains since the end of the War, yet they have found nothing. If General Yamashita had buried gold there, the men would have found some of it by now, or perhaps all of it." She waved her hands delicately as she spoke, but now she folded them in her lap. "Yamashita was hung. Executed for his war crimes." Her voice softened. "He has paid the price for his wrongdoing." She made the sign of the cross, and Tom followed suit. "We must forgive him and move onward toward goodness."

After he crossed himself, Tom faltered, unsure what to do with his hands. Usually in control in both social and business situations, he found himself at a loss. He couldn't find words to speak. He felt himself grow warm, and he looked helplessly at First Lady Quezon.

She offered a smile. "Is your tea warm enough?"

Tom looked down at the teacup. He picked it up and took a long, slow sip, grateful the woman prompted him to the distraction. "It's delicious, thank you."

The first lady watched him for a moment. "Is there something else you wanted to ask me?"

Tom shook his head and worked his mouth, but it was a moment before his voice worked. "No. No, that was it."

Her voice was kind and soft when she laughed. "Do you mean to tell me that the US Government sent the FBI to ask me where war gold was hidden in the Philippines?"

She said where, *not* if. Tom placed his cup in the saucer and set it on the table. He leaned forward. "No, First Lady. The FBI doesn't know I'm here. They did not request or authorize this visit."

She tilted her head in a lady-like manner, her eyes questioning, but kind. "Oh," she said. She did not press for more.

Tom felt his tension loosen its grip, and relieved, he rushed to explain, not wanting her to think he was there as a greedy treasure-seeker to pick her brain for secrets. "A man I worked with—my dear friend—was killed on Montalban Gorge last year when we accidentally stumbled upon a site where men were digging in the ground. We learned they were searching for stolen war gold, and they must have thought we were there to take it from them."

Unabashedly, she scooted forward on her high-backed chair and reached for Tom's hand, patting it and stroking it. "I am so sorry, dear man. That must've been a terrible thing to endure." She gave his hand a final squeeze, then slid backward on her chair. She stared at the photo of her late husband again for a moment, then turned to look at Tom again. "I believe I remember this—this tragedy that happened to your friend. Montalban Gorge, you said? Yes, I recall hearing about that. A brutal event, as I recall."

"Yes," Tom said quietly. "Yes, it was."

"Do you know who the men were who harmed your friend? Have they been brought to justice?"

"No, I'm afraid not." Tom wished now he hadn't come here, hadn't gotten her involved in his quest for answers. He didn't want to appear to be pressuring this philanthropic angel of a woman into helping him avenge Snake's death. Tom cleared his throat again and reached for his tea. "It was foolish of me to ask you, I realize." He softened his voice. "You have a reputation for honesty, First Lady. I knew you would tell me the truth." He bowed his head in deference. "Thank you. Thank you so much."

She smiled sweetly. "I'm sorry I didn't have all the answers you wanted. I expect the men who—who did that terrible thing . . . I expect they were bandits. I'm afraid there are too many rebels who live in the hills surrounding Manila. It was always Manny's—President Quezon's—intent to better police those outlying regions. Alas, he ran out of time." She straightened her spine and pulled back her shoulders, as if a donning a coat of resilience. "May I ask something of you now, Tom?"

He placed his cup and saucer on the table and leaned forward. It surprised him how eager he felt to please this woman. "Of course."

"Tomorrow is a very special day for me and my family." She gazed again at the photo of the late President Manuel Quezon, a happy smile lighting her entire face. "Tomorrow I am dedicating a hospital to my husband's memory." She looked at Tom, her cheeks fairly shining when she smiled. "Quezon Memorial Hospital. In his hometown of Baler."

Tom first shared her smile, then the location dawned on him. "Baler? That means you'll need to go through Luzon."

She nodded, still smiling.

"But that's . . . pardon me, First Lady Quezon, but that will be dangerous."

"Yes," she said, waving her hands as if shooing away flies. "I have been told this many times. It is important for me to do this, however." She lifted her chin slightly. "Besides, my daughter Baby and her husband Philip have arrived to accompany me, just for the occasion. They want to honor their father, as well."

Tom slid forward on his seat. She couldn't realize the grave danger she might face crossing Central Luzon, where the Huk insurgents now frequently instigated roadside attacks.

"I see." He held his palms toward the woman, pleading. "I expect the hospital grand opening has been well-publicized in Baler, yes?"

"Oh, yes. We expect quite a crowd." She blinked rapidly.

"No doubt, then, the Huks know you will be traveling through Luzon tomorrow, if not tonight. They may lay in wait for you."

She offered a soft laugh and gently patted the hair above her ear. "Hukbalahap Supremo Taruc knows my white hair. He will not hurt me." She sipped from her teacup and balanced the cup and saucer delicately on her lap. "Besides, I am taking a whole entourage with me." She tilted her head and smiled mischievously. "And perhaps the American FBI will be part of that support team."

Tom's mouth dropped open, and he quickly closed it and swallowed.

"This is what I wanted to ask you, Tom. I would like you and perhaps a few of your FBI men to accompany my family and me to Baler." She curled her fingers around her cup and saucer, waiting with an expectant smile.

"Respectfully, I don't think you understand—"

"The danger. Yes, yes, there is always danger. Dear man, I have lived amid political danger all of my life. The work of God must go on. The people of my husband's hometown need this hospital, and I must give it to them. It is already planned."

Tom took a deep breath. How could he say no?

"Besides, it will be safer than you may believe. My caravan includes twelve vehicles. Yours will make thirteen." She smiled, placed her cup and saucer on the serving tray and lightly bounced her hands together twice, as if clapping. "Major General Ravael Jalandoni, my late husband's retired Armed Forces Chief of Staff, he will be driving us, and Quezon City Mayor Ponciano Bernardo will be accompanying us. We'll take my Buick, so as not to be pretentious."

Tom blinked. "But you said you had an entourage. Won't that stand out?"

She again waved her hand. "Only as a show of power, if that's really necessary. There will be at least two military jeeps with armed soldiers—the Major

General insists—so we will have plenty of protection, you see. And with you and your men, I feel confident we will arrive safely in Baler."

Tom knew he'd been trapped, but when he thought of what this generous woman was undertaking by driving through insurgent territory, he could think of no place he'd rather be than personally with her to guarantee her safety.

He felt a smile creep across his mouth, matching hers. "I will be honored to accompany you, First Lady Quezon. It will be my pleasure."

⤙═◉ ◉═⤚

Later that night, Dr. Wang's car pulled up to the guerilla hideout. The car doors opened and two Chinese men stepped out of either side, their hands in the air. Several armed men in the woods whistled, and two more gunmen emerged from the small building.

The Chinese men told the two gunmen they had been sent by Manuel Ochua and Guillermo Capadocia, immediately the guns were lowered. One of the Chinese men stepped to the back door of the car, opened it, and a man in a gray suit stepped out, then proceeded inside.

Once inside, Dr. Wang stepped forward. "I am here to speak to Alexander Viernes."

After a few seconds, from another room stepped Viernes. "I understand you have a mission for me, Dr. Wang."

"Yes. Tomorrow there will be a caravan moving through your territory. In that caravan is former First Lady Aurora Quezon, some of her family members and several other dignitaries. Capadocia and I think we can make a political statement and give us great negotiating power with the Philippine government, if we kidnap Mrs. Quezon and her party. You may kill the rest, if you wish. That will be your choice. Do you have sufficient manpower to carry out this operation?

Viernes smiled. "Yes, I do. I am honored that Comrades Taruc and Guillermo have selected me to carry out this raid."

Dr. Wang handed him an envelope. "Here is their route and the size of their entourage. The rest of your instructions are inside. I shall inform Chairman

Mao, Comrades Taruc and Capadocia that you have accepted their mission. Remember, we want them alive. It will provide us great power to negotiate with the Philippine Government." Dr. Wang bowed his head then turned and walked out of the tiny building.

Chapter 25

Central Luzon, Philippines
April 28, 1949

TOM PUT A hand on the dashboard and peered out the windshield. "Where are they?"

Sal rolled down the window and stuck his head out the driver's side window, peering around the two military jeeps ahead of him. "I see them. They're getting a little ahead of the lead Jeep, though. The major general ought to slow down if he doesn't want to lose his motorcade."

Ricky scooted forward and draped his lanky arms over the backseat of the car. "Can you pass them?"

Sal glanced over his shoulder. "No, I can't pass 'em. Get the hair out of your eyes." He returned his eyes to the road and mumbled, "We're in the middle of a mountain jungle. We get one tire off the road here, the bank could break away, and they'd never see us again. Hard to tell where the foliage ends and the dead air begins."

"Why'd they come this way, then?" Tom asked. "Isn't there a better roadway to Baler?"

"The Baler-Bongagon Road is the *only* roadway connecting Nueva Ecija and Luzon to Baler." Ricky leaned into front seat again. "The First Lady herself inaugurated this road back in 1940, before you arrived in the Philippines, boss."

Sal slowed the car again as the motorcade navigated a hairpin turn. "They're almost out of sight," he said. "Who thought it was a good idea to put the first lady out in front, anyway?"

Tom frowned. "If I had to guess, it was probably her own." He strained to peer ahead of the military Jeeps, but couldn't see the Quezon's Buick. "Major General Jalandoni should know better, though."

Sal slammed on the brakes. "What in the—" The caravan had stopped. "This isn't safe, boss."

Tom rolled down his window and leaned out, looking ahead, then behind him. "I think the first Jeep stalled up there. I hope that's all it is."

As the driver tried to start the motor it made a grinding sound, and within a minute, the vehicle lurched forward.

"We're moving." Tom tried to keep any concern out of his voice.

"Can you see her?" Ricky asked from the backseat.

Tom leaned out the window again and squinted as exhaust blew into his face. "The major general must not know how to use a rearview mirror. They've driven on, damn it." He sat hard onto the seat and rolled up the window against the dust kicked up by the Jeeps. "I don't feel good about this."

"If those two knuckleheads driving those Jeeps would either speed up or pull over, I could catch her," Sal said. "Think I should lay on the horn?"

Tom reached out a hand to stay him. "No, don't do that. The way our luck is going, they'll think there's a problem back here and stop to check, and we'll lose even more time."

About fifteen minutes later, they crested the top of the mountain, and though the palmettos had given way to scrub pines and woody trees, the underbrush was still too thick to see what lay below. Sal downshifted, and the car groaned beneath its weight as they started down the precarious, curvy slope. Another ten minutes, and they were back into denser foliage, and dusty bushes occasionally clawed at the car as they hugged the jungle to pass the rare vehicle heading in the opposite direction.

They neared another long switchback turn.

A cracking sound—like a gunshot—echoed through the mountains. Then an explosion of many gunshots. Tom struggled to see out the window at the road ahead that lay a few hundred yards below them. "Dear God," he said. "They've been attacked." The first Jeep ahead of them must have seen the attack as well, because suddenly both Jeeps accelerated and raced down the mountain, kicking up a dust storm as they traveled. Sal chased after them.

As they drove down the mountain, they lost sight of the Quezon's Buick, but after a few minutes that felt like an hour, the two Jeeps ahead of them slid to a stop on the dusty road. The soldiers jumped out, but before they could reach the Buick, gunfire exploded around them.

Sal slammed on the brakes, threw the car into reverse and backed it hard up the road about fifty yards and into a stand of palmettos.

"What the hell are you doing?" Tom demanded.

Sal stomped the accelerator, and the body of the car made a metallic screech as branches dug into its side and roof. "Getting cover. And protecting your ass." As quickly as he threw the car into park and cut the engine, the bulky man pushed open his door, shoving it hard to make room for an exit within the underbrush. He whipped out his pistol and aimed over the hood of the car in the direction of the other cars that had now caught up to the military Jeeps.

A rebel wearing a face scarf lurched backward, flinging his gun into the air before he fell to the ground. Sal had killed him.

Tom and Ricky followed Sal's lead, opening their doors against the shrubs and brush. Crashing sounded in the underbrush several yards ahead of them, and Tom's mouth opened in alarm. He waved over the roof of the car to Sal and Ricky, indicating they should get back in the car. "We have to get down to Quezon's car!" Tom yelled.

"As soon as they were inside the car, Ricky said tersely, "It's suicide, if we go down there!"

"Hundreds of them," Sal said, breathless. "Coming out of the jungle over there. Rebels. Huks, maybe. Hell, I don't know who they are. It's an ambush. We don't stand a chance."

"We have to get to First Lady Quezon." Tom said. "We're here to protect her."

A fresh flurry of gunfire sounded below them.

Ricky gripped Tom's shoulder from the backseat as pops of gunfire echoed down the road ahead of them. "We don't." His voice sounded throaty and grim when he spoke. "It's too late."

"What do you mean it's too late?" Tom asked, his eyes wild.

Ricky shook his head. "I mean, it's too late. All that gunfire . . . who knows how long the shooting went on before we arrived? She's dead. They're all dead."

Chapter 26

Manila, Philippines
June 10, 1949

Tom hung up the phone, his lips pressed together. He stared at his hand on the receiver, as if it was a foreign object.

"Who was that, boss?" Ricky asked. "You look like you've seen a ghost."

Tom released the phone receiver, closed the file folder in front of him, and shoved it to the side. He looked across his desk at Ricky, then at Sal, who sat guzzling his fifth cup of coffee that morning. "We gotta go, boys. Get packing."

Sal looked at Ricky, his bushy eyebrows lifting. He said nothing, but instead turned up his coffee cup, guzzling the last dregs.

"Where are we going?" Ricky asked. "And who was that?"

"That was Hoover." He pressed his lips together and looked out the window, mentally searching for an escape. "We're going to Shanghai."

Ricky leaned forward. "What? You gotta be kidding me!"

Sal set down his coffee cup on the edge of Tom's desk atop the folded square of newspaper Tom kept there for that purpose. "You can't go to Shanghai, boss. That's a death wish. Dr. Wang wasn't kidding when he said he would kill you."

Ricky nodded rapidly. "It took us a week to recover after the last beating that man gave us."

Tom shot the two a scathing look. "We have our orders."

Ricky waved his arms in the air. "He said—no, he *promised*—he promised he'd kill all of us if we showed our faces in China again. Have you ever told Hoover that?"

"What good would it do?" He looked Ricky squarely in the eye. "We became expendable the day we signed up for the FBI, and we knew that." Tom glanced at Sal. The man stood, straightened his tie, and picked up the suit jacket he'd draped on the back of the chair. "What time is our flight?"

Tom shoved the file in his desk drawer and slammed it shut. "We're flying out on a US military plane directly to Hong Kong, so we'll be safe that far, at least. We leave in two hours."

Sal nodded morosely, flung his jacket over his shoulder and headed for Tom's office door.

"Wait." Ricky looked incredulous. "Just like that?" He glanced from Tom to Sal and back again. "We aren't even going to try to reason with Hoover? What's he got going on that's so important that we have to go off on some cockamamie jaunt and risk getting killed? Honestly, boss, I think that man tries to throw you to the dogs, sometimes."

Tom ignored the comment, but he'd thought the same thing himself a few times. "He wants T.V. Soong out of Shanghai. Look, Hoover's plan was to get him and Kung both into the US, so that we can see how much money they really have. Both men want their freedom, and Hoover agreed."

"Why doesn't he just leave, for God's sakes? He has a diplomatic passport." Ricky said.

"The ChiComs, particularly Dr. Wang, have been watching him since we took his buddy Kung out. They've kept a close eye on him."

As they walked, Ricky asked, "Well, what's the plan?"

Tom snorted. "You know the drill. We're closest. And I speak the—"

"You speak the language. Every damn language on the planet, yes, I know." Ricky huffed and flipped up the collar on his Hawaiian shirt. "Pack extra bullets, boys. Extra guns and knives, too. I got a feeling this is gonna be a wild ride."

Tom looked around. "I'll brief you on the plane. I have a great idea!"

Ricky just kept walking, shaking his head.

Chapter 27

Shanghai, China
June 10, 1949

TOM TOOK A bite of dry toast from the room service cart and paced again to the open window, staring out half-unseeing at the streets of Shanghai. This time they were staying at a hotel nearest the US Consulate. Below him, a rickshaw fought for space amid other rickshaws, pedestrians and automobiles on the city's crowded street. Already the exodus of businesses had begun, and the city had surprisingly changed for the worse since his last trip here, a result of the People's Liberation Army taking control.

He turned away from the window, nearly bumping into Sal, who'd come to peer out, a cup of bitter coffee in his hand. He pointed to the cup dwarfed by the man's hand. "You're going to eat a hole in your gut if you drink as much of that garbage as you do the good old American joe we keep in the office in Manila."

"Not a bad way to die," Sal grumbled.

Tom paced back to the breakfast cart for coffee and another wedge of toast, intersecting paths with Ricky, who also paced with folded newspaper under his arm as he ate from a saucer of sliced boiled eggs and rice. To say they were all ill at ease would be an understatement.

Tom sat at the tiny desk and opened the operation file again.

T.V. Soong, high ranking Chinese Nationalist Official. Has already transferred bulk of his assets out of China.

Assignment: Get Soong and personal effects out of country before communists occupy Shanghai.

"Damn," Sal said from the window. "He's here."

Tom held a slice of toast by his teeth as he poured dark brew into his cup with one hand and milk into it with the other. He set the pot down and took the toast from his mouth, chewing around his words. "Who? Who's here?"

Ricky pushed a shoulder against the big man to peer out the window beside of him.

"Out there." Sal pressed his finger against the wire screen.

Tom walked up behind the men, then raised on his toes to see out over their shoulders. "Who? Where?"

Sal stepped to one side, furrowed his brow and looked at Tom. "How does he know you're here?"

"Who?" Tom waved his toast.

"Dr. Wang," chorused Sal and Ricky.

Ricky pointed as Tom stepped to the window screen. "There. With those two gunsels. They must be casing the Consulate."

Tom watched as the three men crossed the street and got into a car, forcefully merged into heavy traffic and drove slowly through the crowded street. "I doubt they know we're here."

"How can you say that?" Ricky turned and faced Tom. "They were walking the street in front of our hotel, and they'd parked right out in front."

"If Dr. Wang knew we were here, he'd have kicked in our door already. If he suspected we were coming to Shanghai, then he wouldn't have expected us come in via military plane. Besides, I think he was casing the Consulate   that's all that makes sense." He stuffed the last of his toast in his mouth, chewed and swallowed. "He and his henchmen are probably checking all the hotels in Shanghai. Besides, he left, didn't he? That means he didn't find us here."

"Are you sure he's casing the Consulate? And what if he comes back?" Sal asked.

Tom looked at his watch, calculating the time change in his head. "This time tonight, we'll be out of the country with T.V. Soong safely in our custody."

Ricky still stood by the window. "We'd better be going then, if we plan to make it in this crazy traffic. Looks like it's bottlenecked to a standstill on the big bridge over there."

Sal walked back to the window and peered out. "Is Wang out of sight?"

"Yup," Ricky said. "He turned left at the end of the second block up there."

Tom grabbed his jacket. "Okay, we clear on the plan?" Instead of a restaurant, this time they were going to use a department store to extract Soong. Same drill as with Kung, two get-away cars with two escape options.

"Got it, boss. Let get this over with."

Tom drew a deep breath, like breaking a huddle from calling a play during his college days. "Let's hit it then, boys. If we hustle, we can be out of here before Wang knows we've arrived."

⇢▢◉ ◉▢⇠

Two and a half hours later, with T.V. Soong safely sequestered in the backseat, his identity hidden behind dark glasses and a cowboy hat, Sal turned down the roadway heading toward the airport.

"How much farther?" Ricky asked from the passenger seat.

Sal shot him a scathing look. "Really? You're gonna ask that?" He shook his head. "What a child."

Tom cleared his throat loudly as a warning to the bickering duo. He wanted his men to exude professionalism and confidence to the man sitting beside him—the man who was physically trembling beneath his ridiculous-looking hat. He gave T.V. Soong what he hoped was a look of calm confidence. "We're less than a mile away. We'll all be on the plane to Hong Kong in no time, and from there we'll have you bound for the US within the hour."

Soong bowed his head toward Tom and tried to smile, but his lips faltered and twisted into a pained grimace. "Thank you," he managed.

As they drew closer to the Hongqiao Airport, traffic grew heavier, though the thoroughfare was much easier to navigate than the main streets of Shanghai. The car ahead of them stopped. Several seconds ticked past. Sal beat his fists on the steering wheel, then finally blew the horn. The car ahead inched forward, but only a yard or so, then it stopped again.

Ricky shook his head. "So many people trying to escape the Communists. This is the last open airport."

"Why are we stopping?" Soong asked, his voice high-pitched. He wrung his hands and peered out the windows.

"Someone having car trouble ahead of us, I guess," Sal said.

The car ahead of them moved forward again, but at a much slower pace than they had been traveling. Sal peered around the car, looking for oncoming traffic so they could pass.

Tom leaned forward and spoke into Sal's ear, so as not to worry T.V. Soong. "I don't like this. Let's move it."

Sal floored the accelerator. The car shot into the oncoming lane of traffic. Just as quickly, he whipped the steering wheel, getting them safely back into their lane.

Tom took a calming breath and sank against the seat. False alarm. He turned to smile at Soong.

The back window exploded around them. "Get down!" Tom pressed T.V. Soong's head down and flung himself over the man's back.

Sal yanked the wheel and punched the gas pedal, tearing the rear bumper off the sedan in front of them. He didn't slow down, but instead rushed headlong into oncoming traffic, jerking the steering wheel at the last crucial moment, sending the car lurching off the opposite edge of the roadway, then swerved back on the road, fishtailing but proceeding toward the airport at a high rate of speed.

Car horns sounded all around them. Something hard pressed into Tom's temple, and he managed to turn just enough to see it was Ricky's elbow. Ricky held his pistol in both hands, aiming out the missing back glass.

"I don't see 'em," Ricky said. "But you can bet he's trying to catch us. Don't slow down, Sal. Get us to the plane."

Sal kept the accelerator floored, weaving in and out of traffic.

"Still don't see 'em," Ricky said.

Bullets pelleted the car, and Ricky spun around in the front and leaned over toward the back seat.

"What the—" Tom waited for Ricky to shoot back or assume a shooting position or something. But he did nothing. "Ricky?" Tom shook his friend. "What's you doing?"

"I don't see 'em," Ricky said. "I don't see 'em."

Tom wasn't sure what was going on, but he pushed Ricky away from him and rose to peer out the back window, keeping his hand pressed on T.V. Soong's head. He looked ahead of him as Sal slowed, relieved to see that they'd reached the military gate. Soldiers surrounded the vehicles with guns pointed at them.

Sal pulled out his FBI badge and held it out the window. "FBI!" he shouted as the guard pointed his gun at Sal's head.

"Step out of the car, all of you!" the guard ordered.

They did as they were told. Tom approached the guard with his hands up and said in Cantonese, "We are under orders from Generalissimo Chiang and FBI Mr. Hoover to get Mr. Soong out of the country immediately. There is a US Air Force plane waiting for us."

The facial expression of the guard never changed. He eyed the three FBI agents, then stepped up and saluted T.V. Soong. In broken English, he said, "*You all clear go.*" Then he turned to the other soldiers and told them to lower their weapons.

The agents hustled back to their car, quickly ushered Mr. Soong inside and drove off.

Blood oozed from Ricky's shoulder and saturated his white cotton shirt.

"What the heck?" Tom said. "You get shot?"

Ricky slipped the shirt off his shoulder, examined the wound, and pulled the shirt back on. "Just a flesh wound. Grazed me."

"We'll get you some medical attention once we get on the plane," Tom said.

Sal pulled the car right up to the waiting twin-engine Beechcraft. "What is this, some kind of bomber? I've driven go-carts bigger than that thing."

"I'd happily take a go-cart right now, if it had wings and a motor," Tom said. "Get us out of Shanghai, before Wang finds a way to break into this military installation."

Less than ten minutes later, the engines on the small plane began to turn, and soon the four men and their pilot lifted skyward. In the bucket seat beside of Tom, T.V. Soong still trembled.

"It's okay, Mr. Soong," said Tom. "You are safe now. We'll be in Hong Kong soon, where no one is after you." *Or me.* "Within a couple of hours, you'll be on a nice big plane with pretty stewardesses, heading to the United States of America."

In the seats ahead of him, Sal looked at Ricky. "United States of America," he echoed. "Sounds pretty good, doesn't it?"

"Not bad." Ricky grinned at Sal. "Speaking of not bad, I've gotta say, your driving is getting better all the time."

Sal chuckled, then turned to look out the window.

"Almost as good as Snake's," Ricky said quietly. He sank back into the seat and closed his eyes.

Tom chuckled, then sat back in his seat and closed his eyes. After a minute or two, his eyes popped open. He leaned over toward Ricky and motioned Sal to lean in, then whispered, "There's a security leak in our organization. Dr. Wang and the Huks have been aware of our every move since the day we got to the Philippines. We better to get to the bottom of this before we end up dead."

Chapter 28

Manila, Philippines
March 8, 1950

As Sal drove him across Camp Aguinaldo, headquarters of the Philippine Army and the Armed Forces of the Philippines, Tom was gazing out the window at the barracks at the back of the facility, where they'd been routed to meet with Major Santos. The US Air Force vehicle approaching them stood out amid the Philippine Army Jeeps, and Tom pressed his head against the window, peering to see who was inside as it passed. "That's Colonel Lansdale," he said. "In full uniform."

Sal said, "I didn't know Lansdale was back in the Philippines. Wonder when he got here?"

"I don't know. I talked with Hoover yesterday, and he didn't say anything about his return. Perhaps he was here meeting with Santos, too."

Moments later, the trio walked into the office of Major Santos, where the receptionist delivered the news.

"I am sorry, Special Agent Warren," she said. "Major Santos was urgently called out of the office. You will have to reschedule."

Tom said, "When do you expect him back? We can wait."

"I am sorry, sir. He will not be back today."

Tom shoved his hands into his pockets and walked out of the barracks toward their car. He spoke in a quiet voice to Ricky and Sal. "Well, once again, Santos's vehicle is here. He is avoiding us. Do we think this is related to seeing Lansdale?"

Ricky nodded. "Come on, Sal. Let's see if we can find Lansdale. He is in uniform, and since he's in an Air Force vehicle, he might be headed to Clark Air Base."

When they'd exited Camp Aguinaldo, Sal glanced at Tom in the rearview mirror. "So, now we are adding Lansdale to our tail list? We're already trying to follow Pomeroy; we're working with Candy Man—but we have *nothing* to show for any of it."

Tom pressed his lips together. "I'm aware. Just drive."

Hours later, they still hadn't picked up Lansdale's trail. Tom gave up. "Stop at that market," he said, pointing out the window to a crowded meat-and-fruit stand they'd already passed five times as they'd driven back-and-forth past Clark Air Base. "I'm hungry."

Tom and Ricky selected fresh fruit and a container of rice, while Sal perused the meat stand. Tom paid the vendor. Before they made it to the car, Ricky delved into the bag, pulled a banana from the stalk and peeled it. "You owe me for that," Tom said, feigning a frown.

"Put it on my tab." Ricky downed half the banana in one bite and scanned the street. "Sally get lost?"

"Nah, he's still in the meat market. He'll be out in a jiffy."

Ricky elbowed Tom. "Look." He pointed down the street. "There's Lansdale. We should go say hello." He shot a mischievous grin at Tom.

Tom returned the smile and nodded. "Yes. Let's do that." He chuckled, and the two picked up their pace. They'd only covered a quarter of the block, when Tom reached out with his free hand and grabbed Ricky. The two of them ducked quickly behind a huge display of wicker baskets. "Santa Romana," Tom whispered, as if they could be heard so far away. "A.k.a. Father Jose Antonio Diaz."

Tom and Ricky peered around the basket display as the priest, who they'd learned called himself *Santa Romana* among a small and select political crowd when not in his cassock, walked directly up to Edward Lansdale. The two shared a handshake and clapped each other's shoulders.

Tom squeezed Ricky's arm. "Go intercept Sal, before he stumbles into them. I'll stay here and watch. Have Sal take a picture of this meeting to add to our collection."

Ricky nodded and threaded his way back through the crowded market, quickly disappearing from view.

Someone tapped Tom's shoulder. "You buying, or are you stealing?" said a tiny, flat-faced man in a brown barong tagalong.

Tom pointed around the baskets. "I'm watching someone." He pressed a finger to his lips, pulled out two American one-dollar bills, and handed them to the man.

The little man beamed and waved the bills in the air. "Watch all you want!" He bounced away in short, close steps, causing Tom to shake his head.

Tom turned his attention back to Lansdale in time to see the two men part ways. Why had they met in the marketplace? Did something change hands? Tom cursed under his breath as Lansdale walked away from the priest with a spring in his step. He looked for Santa Romana, then realized the man stood partially hidden between two vegetable carts, staring after Lansdale. Santa Romana watched Lansdale until the colonel became lost in the crowd, and then a smile snaked across the man's face—a smile so wily it caused a chill to race across Tom's neck. Santa Romana turned and ducked into an alley.

Tom quickly hustled across the street, dodging a group of children chasing a small barking dog. When he reached the entrance to the alley, he lifted the grocery bag in his arm to hide his face, peering over the top. Santa Romana was nowhere to be seen. "Where did you go?" Tom muttered. "Man's like a ghost."

Twenty minutes later, Tom placed the bag of fruit on his desk in the FBI office and turned toward Ricky. "Get on the telegraph. Send a message to Willoughby to stay by the phone. I'm going to call him within the hour."

"Boss," Sal said, "it's only five in the morning in the US."

"Damn it." Tom ran his hand through his hair, then yanked his necktie to loosen it. He looked at Ricky. "Okay. Send a telegram telling him to call me as soon as he's available." He looked at his watch. "He'll be in by what? Seven, eight? That gives us a couple of hours." He pressed his lips together, then looked at Sal. "Let's all head back to the apartment complex. You can cook those steaks for our dinner."

Chapter 29

TOM SAT AT his desk in the FBI office, glancing often at his black telephone, willing it to ring. He tapped his pencil until Sal reached out a hand from across the desk to stay him.

"Sorry, boss. You're driving me nuts with that." He held up his hand in peace.

Tom nodded and pressed his lips together. "I've got to have answers this time. I feel like I'm playing pin-the-tail-on-the-donkey blindfolded, but there's not even a donkey on the wall." He let out a heavy sigh. "I hope we get a good overseas connection this time. The last few times I've talked with Willoughby, our calls have dropped, and I couldn't get through again."

Sal looked at Ricky, and Ricky's eyebrows rose skyward. Ricky fumbled with a button on his Hawaiian shirt.

"What?" Tom asked.

Sal shrugged, so Tom glared at Ricky "What? What is it?"

Ricky's shoulders drooped. "I don't know, boss. It just seems that . . . it's funny your calls to Willoughby always get dropped when you ask him a question he doesn't want to answer. That's all."

Tom's jaw twitched. "It's an overseas call, Ricky. You know how those connections are. They're terrible."

Ricky glanced at Sal, then looked at Tom. "Does it happen as often with Hoover?"

"Well . . . no . . . but—look, it's probably the time of day we talk or something. Or maybe those overseas operators, you know, they work harder to keep the connection if the head of the FBI is on the line." He ran his fingers through his hair, then smoothed it back into place. He scowled at Ricky. "Don't read into it, okay?" He stretched his neck and straightened his tie for the hundredth time that day.

Ricky and Sal exchanged an "I told you so" look, then Ricky stood and walked to the window, staring out at the dark street.

The phone rang. Tom startled, but quickly answered. "Special Agent Thomas Warren."

Ricky hustled back to his seat across from Tom and leaned forward, his elbows on his knees.

"Yes, sir," Tom said into the receiver. "No, sir, I wouldn't have asked you to call unless I felt it was important . . . yes, I realize overseas calls are quite expensive. I'll keep it brief."

Sal shook his head.

"Yes, sir. I saw Colonel Edward Lansdale yesterday. I didn't realize he was back in the Philippines. I haven't had the opportunity to speak with him yet, and I didn't want to come across to him as ignorant. I was wondering, sir, if you can share with me why he is back here."

Willoughby raised his voice so loud that, despite the distance and the communication delay, Tom had to hold the phone an inch from his ear to keep from being deafened as the man spoke.

"If you'd been doing your job, Tom, Lansdale wouldn't be there. President Elpidio Quirino personally called President Truman and requested Lansdale's presence to put an end to the Huk Rebellion. He's getting ready to show you up, boy. I suggest you and your playmates get off your asses and squash those damn Commies before Lansdale steals your thunder."

Tom took a deep breath. "Yes, sir. We're working on it, sir. Getting closer every day. You have my word." He hesitated, then took a chance. "By the way, in 1944, you arrested Taruc and Alejandrino. However, there's no information about that in Hoover's report. Can you get me that information, including who might have interrogated them?"

"I'll look around and see if I still have that," Willoughby said, his voice gruff. "Nothing important."

"Sir, can you shine any light on Colonel Lansdale's relationship with a man named Santa Romana?"

Static filled the line, followed by silence. Tom pressed his lips together, worried he'd lost the connection. "Sir?"

Ricky leaned forward and whispered, "Ask him about Dr. Wang."

Tom waved him away.

Ricky stood, stalked toward the window and stared out.

Tom shook his head at Sal. The man was right; Ricky did sometimes act like a teenager.

"Who did you say?" Willoughby's voice grew terser.

"Santa Romana. He also goes by the name of Father Jose Antonio Diaz, often dressed as a priest." Tom propped an elbow on his desk and leaned his head against the phone receiver as Willoughby spoke.

"You're questioning Lansdale's relationship with a *priest?* If the colonel wants to pray, let the man pray. And by the way, I don't know, nor never have heard of, Santa Romana. Stay out of it, Tom. I'm warning you. If you were as concerned with the Huks as you are with Lansdale, this insurgency would have ended by now."

"We are on the verge of several breakthroughs," Tom snarled. "That is, *if* we could just get some cooperation. We are currently tailing William Pomeroy, surely you remember him—he was assigned to General MacArthur during the War—he is working with the communists. Can I get any of your files on him?"

Willoughby said, "Pomeroy, Pomeroy, I don't believe I remember him. I will check my files. Now go get those Huks." The line went dead.

Tom slammed down the phone. He drummed his fingers on the desk, then turned and faced him men. "I think I hit a nerve." He let out a deep breath. "C'mon. Let's go pick up Pomeroy. We need to accomplish something today."

Tom pressed his lips together. He stalked toward the door and yanked his suit jacket from the coat tree. "I'm beginning to think Snake was right about Willoughby."

"What's that?" Sal stood and followed Ricky and his boss to the door.

Tom turned off the light. "There's more going on here than meets the eye, and Willoughby is clearly part of it."

They drove around town, checking the areas where Pomeroy was known to hang out. After forty-five minutes of driving, Ricky waved frantically. "There!"

Tom spotted William Pomeroy, the American journalist whom Huk leader Luis Taruc had hired to write his biography. The man was running pell-mell across the unlit street heading straight toward the priest. Father Diaz smiled as Pomeroy approached.

Santa Romana was dressed in a cassock in his Father Jose Diaz persona.

"They're making an exchange," Ricky said.

"An exchange?" Tom leaned forward, resting his arms on the front seat.

"Yes, sir. William Pomeroy just handed Father Diaz a large, thick packet. It looks like a sheaf of papers, and it's wrapped in paper and tied with string."

Santa Romana took the packet and quickly walked off.

Sal pulled the car forward without being prompted, but though he reached the intersection within seconds, Santa Romana was nowhere in sight. "Okay," Sal said, "I guess we follow Pomeroy."

Tom said, "Here's our chance, let's pick up Pomeroy now. I want to question him."

Sal pulled the car to the side of the street, and each man jumped out and started after Pomeroy. The second Pomeroy saw them coming, he ran. Within minutes, the old man managed to allude the FBI.

Chapter 30

Manila, Philippines
June 21, 1951

TOM THREW HIS cards on the small kitchenette table of his apartment. "I fold." He lifted his glass and swigged the last shot, then refilled his, Ricky's and Sal's glasses as Sal scooped his winning chips from the center of the table.

"Next bottle's on me." Sal grinned.

"It'll have to be," Ricky said. "At this rate, I'll be broke before my next pay day arrives."

"You deal." Sal tossed the deck to Ricky. "I gotta stack my chips." He snickered.

Tom frowned and rubbed his corrugated forehead.

"What's wrong, boss?" Ricky asked as he dealt the cards for another game of five-card draw. "You look worried, and I know it ain't one losing hand that's causing that face."

Tom raked together his pile of cards, but left them laying in front of him as he stretched his arms overhead and arched his back. He let out a long sigh, then picked up his cards. "No, I'm good. No worries here."

Sal shot a look at Ricky. "Probably putting up with you is making him nutso."

Ricky put down the remainder of the deck and picked up his cards. "He never stressed like this until you joined the team, Salvador."

"Finally," Sal said. "You learned how to say my name. Maybe a few years from now, if you practice hard enough, we can teach you to write it." He scowled. "Ignorant jerk."

"Who are you calling a jerk?" Ricky asked, raising his voice.

"Oh," Sal said, smirking. "So you're okay with being called ignorant?"

"Guys," Tom said, "enough."

Ricky's lower lip protruded, and Sal hunched forward, his big shoulders creating a cavern over his chips.

"Sal, did you learn anything new at mass yesterday?" Tom asked.

Ricky snickered.

Tom shot him a warning glance. "I mean, did Father Diaz do anything out of the ordinary?"

Sal shook his head. "You know, boss, at heart, I believe he's serious about his priesthood. He's convinced me that he believes in God. He's a devout man of faith." He waved his thick fingers over the table. "I can't vouch for him yet, but I'd say he certainly has a good side."

"Bullshit," Ricky said.

"What did you say?" Sal's face reddened and he drew up his torso, dwarfing the other two men at the table. "You doubting a priest's love of God?"

Tom slammed his fist on the table. "Stop it!" He flung his cards on the table. "I'm sick of you two and your arguing!" He jumped up from the table, tipping over his chair. "Either shut the hell up, or get out!"

Ricky's gaze found the floor, and he looked up at Tom from beneath a fringe of eyelash. "I'm sorry, boss. *We're* sorry."

"Yeah," Sal said. "We're very sorry." He slid back his chair without standing. "You want us to leave, we'll go."

Tom paced the floor and huffed. He held out his hand toward the men. "No, don't go." He blew out another puff of air. "Look, I'm the one who should be apologizing."

"You getting another migraine?" Ricky asked quietly.

Tom shook his head and grimaced. "No, but that doesn't mean my head doesn't feel like it's going to pop off." His face felt hot, inflamed. "It's just—I'm at wit's end, boys." He paced to the window, looked out, then jerked the curtains together, blocking out everything below. He stood there, his hands still gripping the curtains, and his shoulders sagged. He released them and shook his head, then he straightened and turned back to Ricky and Sal.

"I'm just sick of it, guys. I'm sick of the Philippines, sick of being away from the US, sick of the damn FBI, sick of the lies and secrets . . . I mean . . . I used to be a college athlete, and today I couldn't catch that old man Pomeroy." He took a deep breath. "I want out. I really want out." He paced the floor in long strides. "I know—you don't have to tell me—I can't leave until we put an end to the Huk Rebellion."

Ricky and Sal looked at each other with round, sorrowful eyes, but neither spoke.

"You know, we could squash this thing and get out of here a hell of a lot sooner if Major Santos would cooperate with us on the Philippine side." He flung an arm in the air. "But he won't. Why won't he? It makes no sense. We both want the same thing here. What a stooge." Tom shook his head and puffed air through his nose. "And to make matters worse, I'm always looking over my shoulder for dear Dr. Wang, and right now—right at this very moment—he could be anywhere—and he always seems to be a step ahead."

Tom jabbed a finger toward the closed curtains. "He could be right out there with his gunsels, staring up at this window." He paced over to his two agents and threw his hands in the air.

When Tom grew quiet, Ricky softly cleared his throat to break the silence. "Maybe you need some time off, boss. Take a vaycay to the US of A. Go see Judy. Get a little R and R, maybe some fine loving with Miss Judy while you're there." He offered a smile.

Tom glanced back at Ricky, stared at the wall, then looked again at Ricky. "Judy and I broke up last year."

Sal's mouth opened, but he didn't speak.

"I—I didn't know." Ricky's face colored.

"She got married." Tom's voice sounded flat, emotionless, even to his own ears.

As usual, Sal didn't mince words. "You've burned a lot of bridges, haven't you, boss?"

Tom whipped around and shot a scathing look at Sal. He pressed his lips together and turned away. When he looked back, his face was placid. "Yes," he said. "Yes, I have."

Chapter 31

Manila, Philippines
April 14, 1952

TOM STRAIGHTENED HIS tie and brushed non-existent lint from the sleeves of his best suit. He jutted out his chin, put on a confident smile, then rounded the corner and stepped into Major Santos's office. "Good afternoon, Major," Tom said, taking care not to look the man directly in the eye. Such an action was considered an antagonistic gesture in the Philippines. Instead, he looked at the man's portly double chin and broad neck, allowing his gaze to occasionally venture as far north as the large, dark mole beneath his left eye.

"Agent Warren," the man said thickly, pursing his lips toward a leather-padded armchair in front of his cluttered desk. Stacks of folders, papers, thick files and rubber-banded piles of envelopes covered the desk surface. Santos moved one of these paper stacks to see Warren better, or perhaps to keep Warren from seeing what was written on the papers there.

"Thank you, Major." Tom sat, the leather creaking beneath him.

"I have little time, Agent Warren. No time for small talk. Get to the point, please."

Tom's jaw twitched. "Yes, sir. Simply put, sir, I'd like the two of us to work together. We both want to squelch the guerilla insurgents and disband the Communist Hukbalahap, and I believe—"

"No," Major Santos said tersely.

"Excuse me, sir?"

"I said 'no.' I believe you heard me."

"Sir, if you will allow me a moment to explain, I believe I can help you, perhaps more than you can help me."

The major looked Tom up and down, finally settling his steely stare on Tom's eyes.

Oh, yes, he's aggressive. Tom calmly met the man's intense look without blinking.

"What do you think you can do to help *me*, Agent Warren, that your own Colonel Lansdale and President Truman have been unable to do?"

Lansdale. Tom wasn't expecting to hear Santos admit he was working with Lansdale "Sir, I can hand you crucial information that you currently do not have. Information regarding the Huks, as well as information about an exchange of money and facts that your Panay Task Force will find helpful."

The man continued to visually examine Tom, as if he could probe Tom's secrets with own his eyes. "What do you want out of this exchange of information, Agent Warren?"

"Simple. I want out."

"Out? Out of what?"

"Out of the business of trying to quell these guerilla factions. Out of the Philippines. Perhaps out of the FBI." To hell with acquiescence. Tom maintained eye contact with the beady-eyed man. "You've been to America, to New England, or Arizona, or wherever. That's what I want. I want to get back to the American lifestyle I grew up with."

The major's lips twitched, and his eyes glittered. Finally, a slight smile curved his mouth. "The American lifestyle. Yes, I can see where one who grew up amid such privilege would miss it here."

The tightness in Tom's chest loosened. "Yes, sir."

Major Santos continued to stare as a full minute ticked past on the small gold clock on his desk. "Agreed," he finally said.

Tom turned his ear toward the man. Had he heard him correctly? "You agree?"

The man pursed his lips and gave a jerking nod. "Yes. Tell me what information you have for me."

Tom allowed himself a sly smile. He knew he'd have to make the first move, prove himself to the major, so he didn't hesitate. "First, Major Santos, I have proof that the Huks were behind the ambush of First Lady Quezon's entourage."

"Proof? What kind of proof? Viernes claimed he carried out the attack!"

The image of hundreds of rebels storming down the mountain and surrounding the motorcade flooded Tom's mind, and he couldn't stop the grimace that flitted across his face. "I was there."

The major's slitted eyes opened wider. "You? You were there?"

"Yes, sir. Along with two other FBI agents. First Lady Quezon specifically requested that we join her entourage, but they got ahead of us by quite a distance, and when we caught up to them, the attack had already occurred." He swallowed against the stricture in his throat. "One of my agents got us out of there, but not before we saw at least a hundred guerilla insurgents storm the caravan. I recognized some of them as Hukbalahap. We both know Viernes is a lieutenant, and he wouldn't carry out anything like that without orders from Taruc or Capadocia."

Major Santos sucked in a deep breath. "Luis Taruc testified the Huks were not involved. He gave me his word. He said if he discovered that any of his people had covertly done this horrific thing, he would bring them directly to me."

Tom reached into his suit jacket and pulled out the photographs Sal had taken—photos of Taruc talking with Bill Pomeroy, the American writer. He laid them on the desk in front of Major Santos without speaking.

Santos frowned and leaned forward. He picked up the photos, studied them one at a time. Then he shrugged. "Who is this man? He is an American, yes?"

"That's right, sir. His name is Bill Pomeroy. He used to be an American soldier and worked for General MacArthur and maybe with Lansdale, when Lansdale was a captain. He is an American reporter, but that's not why he is talking to Taruc."

Tom again reached into his jacket, this time pulling out a fold of papers—notes stolen by Candy Man. "This, sir, should be all the evidence you need. These are notes that prove that Pomeroy is writing Luis Taruc's memoir—a memoir in which Taruc boasts about helping the Communist Party of the Philippines."

Major Santo's jowls trembled and his face flushed red. He looked at Tom, his eyes darkening as he spoke. "I will put a stop to this." He stood, and the medals affixed to his khaki uniform shirt shifted with his movement. "If you get more information, let me know," he said gravely. He extended a hand toward Tom.

Tom blinked, surprised at the man's offer of a handshake. He quickly thrust out his own hand. "I am sorry to bring you this news, but I know the Philippines will be stronger because of the way you will handle this problem." Tom tilted his head forward in deference. "Thank you, Major Santos. I look forward to working with you."

Tom walked out of the major's office, but before he was out of earshot, he heard the man's fist hit his desk.

"Luis Taruc," said Santos, his voice thick with rage, "you will regret that you lied to me!"

Tom smiled and stretched his neck, then strolled out of the building. One step closer to going home.

--->=== ===<---

As Candy Man drove through his family's plantation, he made a concerted effort to imagine the wealth he would soon have, but instead, he grew more melancholy. He couldn't staunch depressing thoughts about his failed efforts to fight the Japanese during the war, nor the death and destruction that had consequently come to the islands. Luis Taruc and Guillermo Capadocia now wanted to bring a socialist government to the Philippines. He had hurt his old friends, and now he could hardly face them.

His association with the Americans had certainly not been good for him. They hated him, yet they continued to use him for information. As he drove, he had the sense of being followed. Several times, he pulled off the road but no one passed. He was becoming more paranoid and distraught.

In a small church in Montalban Gorge, Candy Man entered, genuflected, dipped his fingers in holy water and made the sign of the cross. Then he entered the confessional. He spoke quietly. "Forgive me, Father, for I have sinned."

"When was your last confession?" Father Diaz responded.

"It has been a long time, Father."

"What do you wish to confess to the Lord?"

"I have betrayed my friends and my cause."

Chapter 32

Manila, Philippines
April 10, 1952

TOM OPENED HIS eyes and listened. Maybe he'd dreamed the noise. He closed his eyes, but the knock at the door grew louder, more insistent. He threw back the covers, grabbed his revolver and padded barefoot toward the door. He checked through the peephole, then rolled his bleary eyes when he saw Ricky standing there.

He opened the door. "Look, Ricky, I told you and Sal I didn't want to play poker tonight. I need some rest." He kept his hand on the door, blocking Ricky's entrance.

Ricky thrust a folded piece of paper toward him. "I didn't play poker, either. I realized I'd left my badge at the office, so I went back, and this telegraph had arrived."

Tom swiped his hand over his face and swung open the door. "This couldn't have waited?"

"No, boss. I think you should read it now."

Scratching the stubble on his chin, Tom walked over to the sofa and sat down. He unfolded the telegram. "It's from Izzy." He read it aloud.

"Have Wang information [STOP]
"Life or death [STOP]
"Come immediately [STOP]
"Please [STOP]"

Tom continued to stare at the telegraph. Finally, he stood and took a deep breath. He looked at Ricky and raised his eyebrows.

"No. No. You can't do that," Ricky said. "You're crazy if you go back over there."

"Don't worry. I have no intention of going back to Hong Kong."

A relieved smile broke across Ricky's face. "Oh, thank God. I was afraid . . . well, I'm glad you have better sense." He started toward the door. "You need me to go back to the office and send a response?"

Tom waved him away. "Nah. It can wait until morning. Thanks, Ricky." He followed him to the door. "See you in the morning."

An hour later, Tom still tossed and turned, unable to sleep. He'd done the right thing, hadn't he? Of course, he couldn't go back to Hong Kong. He couldn't ask Ricky and Sal to go with him, either. And how did he know Izzy wasn't setting him up? After all, Dr. Wang had been in the lobby of her hotel the day after he'd order his men to pound Tom to a pulp. Santa Romana had been there, too.

Life or death. Whose life—his, or hers? No. No, it couldn't be that cut-and-dried, not with Wang involved. And Wang certainly must be involved. It must be a trap. Well, he was no fool. He wouldn't be led into the lion's den. He'd telegraph Izzy tomorrow that he couldn't make it. Let her deal with that the best way she could.

Tom punched his pillow in an effort to fluff it and yet again rearranged his blanket. He closed his eyes, willing himself into sleep.

Judy floated toward him, her feet nearly a yard above the flower-strewn pathway. Her snowy gown blew in the soft breeze; a wedding gown. A gauzy veil covered her face, but it didn't matter. He knew it was her.

Behind her, a snake rose up, hooded, like a cobra. It swayed back and forth above her head. He called out to warn her, but she didn't turn, didn't stop floating toward him at that agonizingly slow pace. Fog swirled around her, growing thicker and thicker.

She raised her hands to lift her veil, and the snake grew taller. It now wore a man's suit. A gray suit. The snake picked up speed, swaying faster and faster as Judy lifted her veil higher and higher. The snake shed its hood, revealing its face. It was Willoughby.

Judy lifted her veil, and before Tom could see her face, she turned to soot and fell to the ground. A pile of gray ash.

Willoughby smiled at Tom and reached into the dense fog at his side. He pulled a fiery-haired woman out of the thick mist. Izzy Scarborough.

Izzy turned to whisper in Willoughby's ear, but he again shed his skin, revealing the face of a cobra. The cobra bared it's long, golden fangs and bit into Izzy's pale neck.

Tom's own screams woke him, and he jerked up in bed, covered in a slick film of sweat. He staggered to the bathroom, toweled his face and chest, then went into his living room and sat down by the telephone. He picked up the phonebook and flipped it open to the Philippine Airlines. "I need your help, please. I need to arrange for the first available flight to Hong Kong."

Chapter 33

Hong Kong, China
April 11, 1952

TOM GRIMACED WHEN he saw MI-6 Agent Anthony Middleton seated on the padded leather bench outside Izzy's penthouse suite. Once again, he wore an expensive-looking tailored suit, but it looked like he'd slept in it. He stood when Tom and his men approached.

"I've been waiting for you, right?"

Tom felt the muscles in his shoulders tighten. "What makes you so sure I'd show up?"

The man gave a wry smile. "You are not so foolish as to stay away."

"We'll see about that." He extended a hand, and the two shook, then Ricky and Sal exchanged handshakes with Middleton.

"Miss Scarborough is waiting to see you." Middleton gave a rapid knock at the double doors, and Izzy's doorman immediately swung open the doors, as if he'd been standing there waiting. The four men walked in.

Tom looked around. A painting he didn't remember seeing hung on the wall opposite him, but other than that and the fresh floral arrangements decorating the room, nothing had changed since his last visit.

Izzy swept across the floor toward him. He was surprised to see her wearing an emerald green business suit. Despite her professional demeanor, all he could notice was that the color set off her flaming red hair. Her usual Mona Lisa smile was replaced with a strained one, and she quickly kissed his cheek. "Thank you for coming." She nodded and mouthed a quick *thank you* at Ricky and Sal, then looked at Agent Middleton. "Would you gentlemen mind waiting here?"

Tom stepped inside with her. As soon as the door was closed, she gave him a quick peck on the cheek. "I must make a phone call to set up a meeting. We are expected." Izzy hurriedly exited the room.

When she returned, she carried a large briefcase, which she handed to Tom. He followed her, hustling to keep up, as she quickly walked back into the area of the penthouse where the others waited.

Ricky raised his eyebrows questioningly.

Tom shrugged and handed the briefcase to him, then hurried to catch up with Izzy.

Izzy continued on to the elevator and rang the button. The men followed her, like baby ducks following their mother. The elevator arrived, its heavy doors opened by the bellhop, who stepped aside to allow the group to enter. As soon as they were inside, she turned to Tom. "I have a car waiting to take us to our meeting." Her eyes darted to Ricky. "Don't let that briefcase out of your sight."

They all exited the elevator and strode across the lobby to the waiting chauffeured car. The driver opened the door as all of them squeezed inside. They headed for the banking section of Hong Kong.

After traveling several blocks, the driver pulled up to the bank and parked along the curb. He opened Izzy's door, and all of the men followed her out of the car.

They entered the bank lobby. "Tom, carry the briefcase, and come with me," she said quietly.

He did, and the other men sat in the lobby while Tom followed her. She led him down a hallway and into an office. In it sat a heavy-looking, ornate white desk with gilt trim, and to one side a matching rectangular conference table. A man with greasy hair and severe eyebrows sat at one corner of the table. He wore a black suit, white shirt and black tie, but despite his spotless attire, he struck Tom as slimy.

Izzy motioned for Tom to sit, and she took the high-backed leather chair at the head of the table, clearly in command of the meeting she'd called.

Tom scratched his chin. This wasn't what he'd expected to find.

"Special Agent Thomas Warren," Izzy said, "meet Mikhail Gorken."

It was the first time Tom had heard her call him by his name and title, and it sounded strange coming from her mouth. In fact, her voice sounded strange, clipped and tight, instead of the lyrical purr to which he'd become accustomed. He found himself staring at her as if she were a stranger to him.

"Mr. Gorken is a banker from the Soviet Union." Izzy clasped her hands and placed them on the table in front of her. "He will answer any questions you have, Agent Warren." She stared at Tom, slightly tilting her head forward, prompting him to bring up Wang, no doubt.

Tom looked at the man. He'd come this far. What did he have to lose? *Life or death.* He looked at Izzy, then took a long breath. Tom reached into his suit jacket and pulled out a photo, placed it on the table and pushed it toward the banker.

Gorken picked up the photo, and a slick grin crossed his face. He laid it back down. "Yes?"

"Tell me what you know," said Tom.

The man lifted a shoulder. "He goes by Dr. Wang."

Tom pressed his lips together and rolled his eyes. "Everyone knows that." He looked at Izzy. "You think I came all the way from the Philippines to play games?" He glared at the man. "Tell me something I don't know."

The man's brow furrowed, and he shifted on the leather chair. "He goes by another name, Lieu Xu-Jiang. That, too, is a false name. Like me, he is a banker. This how we met. He works at Bank of Communications."

A banker? That would explain the packet exchanges. They *were* envelopes filled with money, just as Tom had guessed. He decided to act bored, and he shook his head. "This is old news."

The man leaned forward. "Did you know then that Dr. Wang came from a very wealthy family in Old China? One of the wealthiest?"

"I know that," Tom said.

The man snarled then a slight smile flitted across his lips. "He has spent much time trying to find the banker of the Japanese Yakuza. He tries to find the personal banker of Yoshio and Ryoichi. He is not successful."

Tom's stomach tightened. Wang had made no secret that he wanted Tom dead. Could he have been behind the set-up, sending Tom, Ricky and Snake into the Yakuza's hands on the mountain? He set his jaw, spoke evenly, forcing his voice to sound void of emotion. "Why would Dr. Wang want to work with the Yakuza, knowing they were involved in the Rape of NanJing?"

The man nodded eagerly, clearly pleased to finally have something Tom wanted. He seemed just as pleased to parcel it out, however, making Tom beg for it. "He hates the Japanese. Hates the Yakuza. What better way to learn everything about their operations in multiple countries than to be in charge of their money?" He leaned forward. "Maybe he plans to steal from them some day."

Tom reached in his pocket and pulled out another photo. This one, he turned upside down and pushed toward Gorken. He watched the man's face carefully as Gorken turned the photo over to examine it.

Gorken's eyes grew large. He pressed his lips together and turned his face away, staring at the far end of the room. He shut his eyes.

"Tell me about him," Tom said.

The man wouldn't speak. Wouldn't even turn to look at Tom or Izzy. His face drained of color.

Tom looked at Izzy. She raised one perfectly arched eyebrow and glanced at Gorken. She looked back at Tom, her face placid. She pushed back in her chair, opened the briefcase and reached into it without looking. She lifted out a thick, banded stack of money and dropped it with a thump on the table between Tom and Mikhail Gorken.

Five thousand pounds.

Gorken turned and stared at the cash, and his eyes glittered.

The man reached for the money, and as soon as he touched it, Tom grabbed his wrist, gripping it tightly. "Talk."

Gorken lifted his hand from the cash, and Tom released him. The man rubbed his wrist where Tom had squeezed. "That is Father Jose Diaz. He is. . . ." The man lowered his voice to a whisper, though only the three of them sat in the room. "He is rumored to have ties to CIA."

The tightening tug in Tom's stomach returned. "I know this. Tell me more."

"He, too, has another name. Many names. I know of one other he uses most frequently—Santa Romana. He once had gold—many tons of gold—in Dr. Wang's bank." Gorken glanced at Izzy, then looked at Tom. "He has gold bullion in many other banks, as well."

Tom fixed the man in his stare. "Does he have gold or money in *your* bank?"

The man shook his head so vigorously his hair shifted across his forehead. "No. He does not." He briefly glanced again at Izzy. "When I was in West Germany, he once had money in my bank, but no more. He closed the account." He turned his palms upward. "The account wasn't under his own name, but it wasn't an alias of his, either. I believe the name may have belonged to a real man, but I cannot prove this."

"What was the name?"

"It was an American name. Uh, Edward." He closed his eyes as though deep in thought, then opened them and met Tom's gaze. "Edward Lansdale."

Tom's mouth went dry, and when he tried to swallow, he nearly choked. He cleared his throat. "Excuse me," he said, then bit his tongue to regain composure.

Gorken must have approved of Tom's reaction, because he quickly rattled off a list of banks located in various cities and countries. "These accounts are under different names, as well," Gorken said. "I know some of the names, but surely do not know them all."

"Can you recall any of the other names?" Tom asked.

"Yes." Gorken rolled his eyes upward, as if remembering or reviewing a list. "Ferdinand Marcos—I believe he may be a real person, too, in the Philippines. Some are not human names, but perhaps are code names. Alpha-Omega is a name under which he has many, many accounts."

"Can you remember any others?"

The man furrowed his brow, then looked at Izzy and shook his head. "I am sorry. I have told you everything I know."

Tom apprised the man for a moment, then looked at Izzy and gave a curt nod.

Izzy stood. "Thank you, Mr. Gorken. Your help is appreciated." She looked at the money, and Gorken quickly snatched it from the table and shoved it inside his suit jacket as he hustled toward the office door.

Izzy gave Tom a wry smile, and when Gorken walked out, she morphed into her seductive nature, grabbing Tom's tie and pulling him toward her.

Tom pulled away and held up a finger. "Just one moment, please." He jogged out of the room and down the hallway. When he reached the lobby, he motioned for Ricky and Sal. "Did he leave?"

Sal nodded. "Just a second ago. Want me to catch him?"

"I want you to follow him. Don't let him see you."

Sal headed for the door and Ricky sat back down. Tom looked at him and jerked a thumb toward the door. "Go with him. I won't leave until you get back."

Ricky took off after Sal.

Tom started back down the hall toward the office, but before he reached it, a hand shot out of another doorway and grabbed his jacket. Izzy pulled him to her, smothering his mouth with her own. "Let's go back to my place and have some fun. All work and no play makes Izzy a very dull girl." She ran her tongue over his lips. "And I am anything but dull!"

Chapter 34

SHINOBU, ONE OF Kodama Yoshio's henchmen, elbowed his partner, Takaharu. Both men were dressed as bellhops. "There he is!" He pointed at Special Agent Thomas Warren as he stepped out of the hotel elevator, his arm linked with the heiress Isabella Scarborough. "His goons are with him."

Takaharu scowled at Shinobu. "Those two are not goons. They are FBI agents, too." He nodded toward the three men. Miss Scarborough accompanied Agent Warren as far as the concierge desk, then she kissed him goodbye. She watched him until he and his men stepped out of the hotel doors.

"They're gone." Shinobu motioned toward her. "Hurry."

The two Yakuza hustled across the lobby, timing their arrival at the elevator with that of the heiress. They let her step into the car alone, but when the doors had almost closed, they both stepped on aboard.

"Oh!" said the heiress. "Are you new here?"

"Pardon." Takaharu bowed toward her. He smiled broadly and turned to face the closed doors as the elevator began its climb.

Shinobu and Takaharu exchanged a knowing look, and when the elevator passed the eighth floor, the numeral symbolizing the *Ya* in *Yakuza*, Shinobu reached out and pulled the red knob on the elevator panel, causing the car to lurch to a grinding halt.

"What are you—"

Takaharu silenced her with a backhand slap that bloodied her mouth and broke her nose. Her hands went to her face, but Shinobu grabbed them and twisted her to the floor in a flash.

A high-pitched laugh escaped his mouth as he knelt behind the heiress's head, holding both of her hands together as he bound them with the cord he yanked from his pocket. His hands were then free to stifle her pitifully soft screams.

Takahuru quickly straddled her, shoving her bloodstained skirt to her waist with one hand while he unfastened his trousers with the other. It excited him when she wriggled against him, but only for a moment, as he quickly grew frustrated with her struggling and punched her face.

When Takahuru was spent, he exchanged places with Shinobu, but Shinobu didn't have to struggle with the heiress's hands as Takahuru had; she lay compliant, whimpering and gurgling as blood oozed from her broken jaw.

Shinobu finally stood and fastened his pants. He pulled out a handkerchief and wiped blood from his hands. Takahuru pointed to his partner's cheek, and Shinobu rubbed the handkerchief there, then examined it, smiling and shaking his head when he saw it was stained with the woman's blood.

Takahuru then cleaned himself, though he'd have to keep his bleeding hand in his pocket when he left the building. He pushed in the knob to restart the car, and it began its climb upward.

Just before the car reached the penthouse floor, Shinobu produced a switchblade and made certain the heiress would tell no tales. Her gurgling stopped before the doors opened, and Takahuru helped him shove the woman's body out into her foyer. Shinobu pulled a chopstick from his pocket and tossed it onto her chest.

The elevator had already begun its descent when they heard the first shouts. The two men smiled at each other. The Yakuza's message had been successfully delivered.

Chapter 35

Manila, Philippines
August 9, 1952

As they finished their normal breakfast meeting, Tom downed the last of his juice, wiped his mouth and put his napkin on the plate. "Good breakfast. You ready, boys? We've got a lot of paperwork to catch up on today. Let's get to the office, I want to get it out of the way, so we can dig into the Santa Romana connection." He glanced at Sal, who still struggled with the revelation that the priest was indeed involved in a vale of secret money-stashing around the world.

Sal smoothed his tie, then pointed behind Tom. "Boss. Behind you."

Tom turned to see the concierge walk into the hotel restaurant holding out an envelope for Tom.

"This telegram just arrived for you, sir."

Tom thanked the man and tipped him, then headed toward the lobby with Sal and Ricky behind him.

"Who's it from, boss?" asked Ricky.

Tom smacked the envelope against his palm. "From Hong Kong." He grinned. "Probably Izzy wanting to thank me."

"Thank *you?*" Sal raised a thick eyebrow. "Aren't you the one who should be thanking *her* for the information?"

Tom chuckled as he slid into the backseat of the car. "It isn't information she'd be thanking me for."

Sal grimaced. "Sorry I said anything."

Tom sank back into the seat and tore open the airmail envelope. He opened the letter. "It's from MI-6 Tony Middleton."

Ricky laughed. "He'd probably be upset that you called him *Tony.*"

Sal shot Ricky a scathing glance. "Like that would stop you from doing it."

Tom chuckled and read the telegraph. He stared at the paper, and his mouth opened. He closed it. He reread the words, unbelieving.

Ricky threw his arm over the backseat and turned. "What's it say, boss? Don't tell me she needs you back in Hong Kong already."

Tom couldn't answer. His voice refused to work. He held the telegraph out to Ricky, and when Ricky took it, Tom turned and stared out the window, unable to process the passing pedestrians and morning traffic on the busy street.

"What's it say?" Sal glanced from the road to the telegraph and back.

"Oh, no." Ricky shook his head.

"What?" Sal asked.

Ricky cleared his throat, but his voice still came out hoarse as he read, "Izzy is dead. Gorken is dead. Waiting by phone for your call."

Sal slowed the car, braking to a near-stop. "Oh, Boss. I'm—I'm so sorry," he said, looking at Tom in the rearview mirror.

Tom continued to stare out the window.

Izzy.

He'd lain in her bed two days ago.

Life or death.

Fifteen minutes later, Tom sat in the straight-backed wooden chair beside the metal utility desk where Sal worked to place an intercontinental call to MI-6 Agent Anthony Middleton. He'd gotten through twice, only to have the call dropped before Tom could speak to the man, and now Tom's knees bounced of their own accord as his nerves stretched tighter.

"Got him!" Sal, handed the phone receiver to Tom.

"Middleton? Yeah, it's Warren." Tom listened as Anthony Middleton relayed the gruesome details of Izzy's brutal rape and murder. Middleton had to make a formal report of speaking with Tom, Ricky, and Sal, since Izzy's staff last saw her leaving the penthouse with them, but the hotel concierge had already verified that they'd left the hotel while she'd returned to the elevator alone.

Tom's stomach lurched as he passed the phone for Ricky's interview. He buried his face in his hands and rested his elbows on his knees. What Middleton had told him sickened him, and he took deep breaths as he tried to think about anything other than Izzy's tiny, porcelain body raped and battered.

The rush of nausea soon passed, replaced with rising anger. He'd lost Snake to these monsters, and now he'd lost Izzy. *Life or death.*

"I choose life," he said through clenched teeth. He raised his fire-filled head.

Ricky and Sal glanced at each other, passing a look between them that said Tom had lost his mind. "What did you say, boss?" Ricky asked, his voice tentative.

"I want out of this. I want to be done with all of it." His head felt hot, swollen with rage and resentment. "I have no doubt the stolen war gold is at the center of all this. Those bank accounts, the murders, the lies—it's a damned cover-up, is what it is, and I'm tired of being a chess pawn in their game, while the people I care about are brutally murdered." Tom stood, paced the floor, then paused by the window and stared out at the busy street, looking, but not seeing.

Sal cleared his throat. "The chopstick they found—Dr. Wang is at the center of this."

Tom turned, blinked hard and looked at the ceiling. "No. No, I don't think he is."

"You don't?" Ricky asked. "I thought we agreed some time ago that he was at the center of the chopstick murders."

Tom looked at him. They were all aware of the Philippine Bureau of Investigation's probe of the serial killer known as Dr. Wang. But of those in this room, only Tom was aware that Dr. Wang's profile included the burning of the word NanJing into the killing chopstick. "I'm sure it wasn't him."

"How can you—"

Tom held up his hand to quiet Ricky. "A number of things. First, all his victims have been Japanese. Second, and this isn't to leave this room, the chopsticks used in all the previous murders had the word *NanJing* branded into the side." Tom shoved his fists onto his hips and scoured his brain for details he may have missed. "I think it's a copycat. I think someone *wants* us to believe Wang is behind Izzy's death so we'll go after him. That'll get the heat off the real killers, plus put Wang out of commission, killing two birds with one stone." Ricky and Sal watched Tom, their eyes darting about. No one spoke.

Finally, Sal cleared his throat. "Who do you think it could be, then?"

Tom pressed his lips together. "I don't know. But I think I know who would know."

Again, he was met with penetrating stares.

Tom paced again. After a few minutes, he swung around and faced his men. "Set up a face-to-face with Santa Romana and Edward Lansdale. I want to meet with both of them, look into their eyes, push and shove them if I have to until they tell me the truth." He continued to pace, gesticulating wildly as he spoke. "Both of them have bank accounts full of gold. We've seen them together here in the Philippines, where everyone, and I mean *everyone*, spreads rumors of buried gold. Maybe they aren't rumors. And if Santa Romana really is using his priesthood as a means to hide money—Gorken said he was rumored to have ties to the CIA, after all—then we have no way of knowing how deep this really goes." Tom stopped at the window again. "But we do know that Lansdale is somehow involved." He looked over his shoulder at Sal. "Set up that meeting. I want to see them both. Together."

"You can't do that," Sal said. "If they're as involved as you say, they'll kill you, too."

Tom whirled around and stalked toward the desk. "Don't tell me I can't do *anything*," he growled. "Set up the meeting."

Sal looked at Ricky, and Ricky glanced at Tom, then back at Sal. "No," they said in unison.

"Fine. I'll call Hoover." Tom reached for the phone, but Sal put his hand over it.

"We're not trying to be obstinate, Tom. We're trying to save your life."

Tom looked at Sal. A by-the-book man, Salvador had never before referred to him as *Tom*. Now that he had, Tom didn't know how to react. Maybe Sal was right. Tom huffed through his nose. "What if we set up the meeting in public?"

Ricky shook his head.

Sally's mouth turned downward. "You'll be killed in broad daylight."

"What do you expect me to do, then? Stand by, while we get picked off one-by-one?"

Tom looked at both men, then slammed his fist on the table. "We have to change our approach. We have accomplished nothing! We have got to stop pussy-footing around."

Chapter 36

Manila, Philippines
September 15, 1952

TOM PUSHED HIS near-empty water glass toward the young woman who served as the FBI secretarial assistant. "Thank you, Darlene." She filled his glass, then repeated the action with Ricky's glass, but Sal held up his hand.

"No, thank you." He waited until the woman left Tom's office before opening the sealed files she'd delivered.

Tom leaned forward and tapped his pen on the table. "What do we know?"

"I talked with Middleton again," Ricky said. "No new details have surfaced regarding Izzy's murder, but he agrees with you. He doesn't think Wang was the killer, and he concedes that someone wanted to throw suspicion on the man."

"Well, who else wants me dead?" Tom asked.

Sal barked out a harsh laugh. "You want the short list?" His smile was dry. "We know that Kang Sheng ordered Dr. Wang — or Lieu Xu-Jiang—whichever you want to call him—"

"Stick with *Wang*," said Tom. "That's how we best know him." He rolled his hand in the air to prompt Sal to continue.

"Kang ordered Wang to kill you—he has no personal vendetta, otherwise. Since Wang didn't eliminate you, perhaps Kang sent someone else." He shrugged. "That could have been Izzy's killer."

Tom looked at Ricky "You talked with Agent Middleton. Does he have any idea who the killer could be?"

Ricky stared at his notebook, not as if reading, but as if thinking hard.

"Well?" Tom prompted.

Ricky swallowed audibly. "Boss, I don't know how to say all this in the best way, so I'll just come out with it." He took a deep breath. "British Intelligence believes that Izzy was a message."

"A message?" Tom looked at Sal, who wouldn't meet his eyes, but instead glanced at Ricky

"She was . . . her murder was . . . it was a message to you."

Tom's mouth fell agape. "To me? To *me!* Who in hell would send that kind of message? And why to me?"

Ricky opened his hands on the table, his expression both pained and earnest. "Middleton thinks they were initially after you, but when you left, they went for Izzy, as a way to warn you."

Tom looked at Sal, and Sal nodded. "That may be the case, boss, as painful as it is to hear. These people, whoever they are, aren't logical creatures. They're violent. They're vicious, and they're bloodthirsty."

Tom pressed his lips together. He didn't speak.

Ricky lightly cleared his throat. "Violent, vicious and bloodthirsty. Boss, you know who it has to be."

"Yakuza," Tom finally said, the word tasting bitter on his tongue.

Ricky nodded. "That's what Middleton seems to think, too. We know Yoshio has been monitoring Santa Romana, a.k.a. Father Diaz, and the fact that a chopstick was left at the scene of Iz—of the murder—Middleton believes it was a trick to make us think Wang was behind it. Right now, we think Wang is behind the chopstick murders, however, up until now he has always targeted the Japanese, and his chopsticks have always had the word *NanJing* burned into them."

"The Japanese," Tom said. "Because they stole his family's fortune."

"Exactly." Sal propped his elbows on the table and interlinked his fingers. "You know, follow the money—or in this case the gold—and it clearly leads to the Yakuza."

Tom stared at Sal, his eyes opening wide. "That's it!"

"What?" Ricky asked.

"Money is the root of this evil. Money. *Money!* The missing printing press and plates. Money. *Gold!*" He smacked is hands flat on the table. "Dr. Wang has made it clear that he wants his family's gold and his country's gold back. He's keeping an eye on the gold being shuffled around the accounts in his bank, and who knows in how many other banks. He's sending messages to the Japanese."

Sal and Ricky looked at each other and nodded, and a relieved smile crept across Ricky's lips.

"This aligns with everything the Russian banker told us, too," said Tom. "Gorken." Tom looked at Ricky, matched his smile. "We're getting there, boys. We're getting there. We were sent here to finish the Huks. Lansdale came back to finish the Huks, but his priest friend is working *with* the Huks. And everybody is being played for the gold."

"Don't all the Chinese Communists want their gold back?" Sal asked. "I mean, they're working with the Huks—been working with the Huks longer than anyone else, from all I've learned."

Ricky nodded. "That's right, and the Yakuza have already found one gold site, and Snake is dead because we were led into a trap there."

Tom tapped his pen on the table again. "We're definitely on to something." He kept tapping, the steady rhythm coaxing him along as he snapped together more pieces of the puzzle. "Okay, we know Santa Romana and Lansdale are digging around for gold, too." Tom snapped his fingers. "Who is this guy, Ferdinand Marcos, working with?"

Ricky looked at Sal, who scratched his head. "Not sure, but that still doesn't explain the connection between Father Diaz, er, Santa Romana, and Dr. Wang. Why would they be in cahoots? Where does the Japanese Yakuza come into this? You don't suppose this Marcos man could be working with them, do you?"

"They'd be in cahoots because," Tom said, grinning now. "Dr. Wang isn't working with Santa Romana."

Sal shook his head. "But you said Dr. Wang gave an envelope to Santa Romana in the hotel lobby that day in Hong Kong. You said it looked like it probably contained money."

"That's right," said Tom. "Dr. Wang is trying to *buy* information from Santa Romana. He *wants* to work with the man, but Santa Romana is playing with him." Tom nodded and chewed his lower lip. "Yeah, that's got to be it. Why would

Santa Romana and Congressman Marcos want to share *any* of that gold?" He shook his head. "They wouldn't! They'd keep it for themselves."

"What about Ed Lansdale?" Ricky asked quietly.

"Lansdale is working for the CIA, period," Tom said. "But that doesn't mean he is reporting everything he is doing. But the man is loyal to MacArthur." His voice rose with excitement. "He's feeding just enough information back to Truman to keep the man happy, but he's keeping the juiciest morsels for the CIA." Tom pushed back his chair, stood and started pacing the floor. "We need another informant. Candy Man is *out*. For all we know, he may be part of our problem—our leak. Remember, Willoughby endorsed him. And he was one of the original Huks arrested in 1944, but there was never any follow-up. We have never received a drop of information there. Why?" He headed back toward the small table, pointing to the stack of thick folders. "Get the Huk files."

Ricky and Sal shifted through the stack of folders, laid two of them out for Tom.

Tom opened one of the thick files, flipped through the dozens of photos of the Communist Hukbalahap.

"What about Lava?" Sal's thick eyebrows rose.

"Who's Lava?" Ricky asked. Tom grinned. "Jose Lava. Yeah." He shoved photos around until he found the one he wanted, then he stabbed the picture with his finger. "There. That's him. He's a Huk leader who lives in the area where the gold was buried. He is one of the leaders of the Philippine Communist Party. He even ran Taruc's campaign. He may still be working with Taruc, Capadocia and Alejandrino." Tom took a deep breath. "He may have been involved in First Lady Quezon's murder."

Ricky picked up the photo and studied it as Tom bent over the table and continued shuffling through pictures of Huks taken all over the Philippines, and even some that had been sent to them from the US.

Tom pointed to another photo, then another. "See, he's in this one, and in this one. This one with Luis Taruc, too. And here." He shook his head firmly. "This man knows things. He gets around. I'm betting he knows where Guillermo Capadocia is hiding, too." Tom stood straight again, put his hands on his hips. "I want him. Find him."

Tom nodded at Ricky, then at Sal, and a sneer spread across his face. "I'm going to squeeze that little maggot until I wring out of him everything he knows."

→=● ●=←

Santa Romana sipped a cup of tea in Jose Lava's living room. Though they'd calmly discussed the evolution of the government of the new country of the Philippines and the direction that the country should take, when Lava mentioned property rights, the mood suddenly changed.

Santa Romana stared hard at Lava. "Tell me about all of the places gold has been buried on Montalban Gorge. You grew up in this region, and I know you personally witnessed many sites where the Japanese buried treasure."

Lava's eyes widened. "I don't know what—"

"Do *not* lie to me," Santa Romana said, his voice bitter.

"Where did you hear of these stories?" Lava asked softly, his voice tentative.

Santa Romana leaned toward Lava, until his face was mere inches from the man's "It matters not who told me. Your eyes tell me it is true. Now tell me what I want to know. I want you to draw a map of all of the burial sites at Montalban Gorge. If your information checks out, then I shall let you live." He sat upright again, lifted a shoulder in a slight shrug. "Refuse to cooperate, and you will have to deal with me in other ways. Ways you may not find as pleasant."

Santa Romana calmly sipped from his tea as Lava walked over to a small writing desk, picked up a piece of paper and a pencil and began to draw a crude map of the four burial sites that he had witnessed on Montalban Gorge. After several minutes of scribbling, he handed the map to Santa Romana, who studied the map for a minute then put it down on the small table.

"This site is being recovered now," Santa Romana said calmly. "I am aware of these other two sites, but this one here . . . is it at the top of mountain near southwest side of the gorge?"

Lava nodded his head, his eyes bulging. "Yes, I am sure of that site. Look for the rock with this Kung symbol on it, then you will know you are there."

"I will check this out. Then I will be back to discuss our new relationship, understand?" He placed his teacup and saucer on the table, stood, and smoothed his barong tagalong. "Your every move will be watched, until I return."

Chapter 37

Pantay, Philippines
September 18, 1952

TOM FIDDLED WITH the big walkie-talkie, then handed over the set to Ricky, who rode shotgun to Sal, as usual. "That's a good toy, all right, but it's kind of gawky, don't you think?"

Sal met Tom's eyes in the rearview mirror as he threw the car into park and turned off the engine. "I agree, boss. Lieutenant Colonel Santos wants us to carry it, though. He said it's the best way for him and his men to keep in contact with us in covert operations like this."

Tom climbed out of the car and smirked at Sal when he saw the almost shoebox-size handy-talkie slung across the man's shoulder. "Covert. Yeah, that's the first word that comes to mind when I see that thing." He grinned at Ricky over the roof of the car.

The trio headed toward Santos and his group of men, who stood in a knot around their own vehicles that were backed against the heavy foliage in a semi-circle, ready to depart. Santos broke away and walked toward them, and his men all turned and watched, clearly aware of any risk for their leader.

Santos strode over to Tom, his face stoic, if not grave. After introductions, Santos motioned to Tom. "May we speak alone?"

"Of course, Lieutenant Colonel. Congratulations on your promotion, by the way." Tom wasn't sure if the man smiled or scowled.

"My men have confirmed that Secretary General Jose Lava is in his house. It's about a kilometer from here. That's where we'll take him out."

Tom felt his eyes widen. "Santos, my friend, do *not* kill Lava. I need him alive. I want to question him. *Extensively* question him, if you know what I mean."

Santos furrowed his brow so severely it pushed his cap upward. "I thought you wanted him dead, too."

Tom pressed his lips into a thin line. "You want Gillermo Capadocia, yes? You want Luis Taruc, yes? Well, sir, I believe Lava knows where Capadocia's hideout is located."

Santos pierced Tom's eyes with his own. "If we can get Capadocia, the Hukbalahap will fall apart. He is one of the founders of the Communist Party of the Philippines."

Tom nodded. "Yes, sir, that's what I've heard. I agree with you. Lava may be our only chance of capturing Capadocia. We take down one of their pillars, in addition to their secretary general, and the Communist Party no doubt will lose their grip on the Philippines."

Santos continued to stare at Tom for a moment, perhaps gauging his trustworthiness. He finally motioned toward one of his men, whom he stepped toward, whispering in the man's ear so quietly that Tom couldn't hear.

Tom turned his face away in an effort to show the man he honored his privacy and trusted him. Trust, in this operation, meant everything. *Life or death.* Unbidden, the words Izzy had written to him surfaced, clearly printed on the telegraph in his mind.

Lt. Col. Santos cleared his throat, calling Tom back to the present. "Special Agent Warren, this is Emilio Laurel. He will accompany you to Lava's house. I will stay here. Laurel is one of our key interrogators and is very familiar with the Huks. As are they with him." He motioned toward Sal. "Your Agent Marino has one of our radios, and he can reach us at any time, if you need assistance." His expression grew severe. "You may be watched."

Tom met the man's grave expression with one of his own. "Who do think might be watching us? The Huks?"

Santos's mouth drew a grim line. "Trust no one. Be vigilant. Things and people are not always as they seem. In the Philippines, even holy men of God are not to be trusted." He turned and quickly strode back toward his vehicle, leaving Tom standing alone.

Holy men of God? Was Santos referring to Santa Romana? He was a priest, after all, a professed holy man of God. Tom decided he would not ask Santos for clarification. If he'd wanted to—or felt safe enough to—elaborate, no doubt the man would have.

Sal and Ricky approached. "Ready, boss?" Ricky asked. Tom introduced Emilo Laurel to Ricky and Sal.

Tom stared after Santos as his men gathered around him, each close, yet giving him the respectable berth his position commanded. He looked at his own men, agents who felt more like brothers. Tom's stomach tightened. *You're excited, that's all.* He squared his shoulders and lifted his chin. "Let's do this thing."

Chapter 38

TOM, RICKY AND Emilio Laurel continually looked out the windows as Sal navigated the roadways toward Communist Party Secretary General Jose Lava's house. As far as Tom could tell, no one followed them or paid them any undue attention. At last, they turned up the long private drive that led through the woods to Lava's place. Tom pressed his face to the glass, peering into the palmettos and underbrush. He saw no one.

When they pulled near Lava's house, Tom leaned forward. "Cut the engine and drift closer."

"Gotcha," Sal said.

He parked the car, but they agreed to leave the doors slightly ajar, in case they needed to make a quick exit. Sal and Ricky split, each standing to one side of the front door, yet out of sight, while Tom walked right to the door and knocked. Emilio Laurel stood on his heels. Tom breathed a prayer of thanks the door didn't have a peephole.

Lava himself opened the door a scant inch. "Yes?" he asked gruffly.

Tom didn't hesitate. The moment the man spoke, Tom slammed his shoulder and hip into the door, sending Lava flying backward into his own living room. Tom ran in after him, followed by Laurel, Ricky and Sal.

Grabbing the man by the hair at the back of his head, Tom shoved his revolver under Lava's chin. "Secretary General," he growled. "You have something I need."

The man both glowered and trembled, but he didn't speak. Tom gripped his hair tighter and yanked hard, stretching his neck back, causing him to grimace in pain. Tom dug the gun muzzle deeper into the soft underbelly of the man's double chin. Lava's hands slowly rose into the air in an act of surrender. "What you are doing here, you are going to get me killed. I have nothing for you," he said between clenched teeth.

"Yes, you do," Tom said. "You have information. That's what I came for. I want answers."

The terror in Lava's face dissipated somewhat, and Tom relaxed his grip, but still kept hold of the man's hair and kept his gun pointed at him as he led him to the straight-backed wooden chair Sal dragged to the center of the room. Tom shoved the man onto the chair, nearly toppling it. Sal pulled out a length of cord and cinched the man's hands behind his back, while Ricky stood guard, peering out the window from behind the heavy curtain that covered it. Emilio Laurel's heavy boots echoed throughout the house as he searched from room to room.

"You're going to talk to me," Tom growled.

Lava nodded, his eyes bulging.

"Where are the US printing press and plates?" Tom asked.

"I don't know."

Tom pushed the gun deeper into his chin.

"The last I knew of them, they were with President Manuel Laurel. We were told before the Japanese Invasion they were sent to Clark Air Base, but they never got there."

This was easy. Tom kept the gun within a foot of Lava's face, and the man never once took his eyes off it. Tom had to admit, it felt good to be on this side of forceful questioning. "Where is Capadocia?"

"He . . . he has a place . . . hideout . . . it's in the jungle."

"Where?" said Tom.

"I can't t-tell you. They'll kill me."

Tom chewed the inside of his cheek. He'd make Lava do that, but he wasn't ready to untie him just yet. "Apparently, a lot of people want to kill you. Now tell me about the gold."

Lava's look went from fearful to terrified. "You can't . . . you can't get to it. Too dangerous." His eyes bulged again, even though Tom hadn't moved the gun. "There are *spirits*. It is the gold of the spirits!"

"Spirits," Tom said, his voice flat.

"Ghosts!"

Tom smirked. "Yeah, right."

"I have seen one myself. The priest . . . there is a priest who visits the mountain regularly. He goes to pray to appease the spirits who guard the gold. If he doesn't pray over them, they will get restless, and they will leave Montalban Gorge and find and kill those who want to dig for gold."

The priest. Father Diaz! Santa Romana. That's how Santa Romana was getting the gold out of those tunnels the Japanese had blasted shut. He'd been the one who started the rumor about evil spirits—probably even set up a hoax to scare away men like Lava—and now the treasure hunters were too terrified to go to the Gorge. And those who did. . . .

Tom remembered Snake, how when he picked his friend up, his body was so badly beaten that the bones folded opposite of their joints. Renewed anger surged through him. "Where is Capadocia now? Is he at the place you just told me about?"

Lava glanced toward the wall, and Tom's eyes followed his gaze. Lava looked at a clock.

"Yes, he will be there."

"Why are you so certain?"

"Because he is meeting with Luis Taruc there in three hours," Lava said.

"Fine. You can take us there!"

"No!" Lava snarled. "I will not betray my comrades. They will kill me! He will torture me to death. Please."

Laurel now stood beside Tom, his gun in his hand by his side.

Tom pressed his lips together. "Lieutenant General Santos and his men are with us. Outside. You can turn yourself in to Santos for protection."

Tears formed in Lava's eyes, but after a moment, he nodded.

Tom glanced at Laurel. "Radio Santos. Tell him I have Lava, and I have the answers I need regarding Capadocia and Taruc. He's all his."

Laurel gave a curt nod. "I will step outside." He took the radio from his shoulder and held it up. "Reception."

As Laurel stepped out, Tom whispered to Sal. "Watch him."

Sal nodded and moved to the window on the opposite side of the door from Tom. He parted the curtain with a thick finger and peered out.

Ricky made a whistling noise to get Sal's attention. "You see him? He stepped out of my range."

"Yeah," Sal said. "He's turning in circles, walking across the road. Think he's trying to get reception." He shrugged the shoulder from which his own handy-talkie hung. "Figured these things were too good to be true."

Tom glared at Lava. "Pen and paper. Where do you keep them?"

"Over there." He tilted his head toward the small table from where Ricky had retrieved the wooden chair. "Top drawer."

Tom glanced at Ricky, but kept his gun trained on Lava's face. "Get it. This man has a map to draw."

Ricky returned with the paper and pen. "Untie him." Tom pressed the gun muzzle against Lava's forehead. "Don't try any funny business, either. I will *not* hesitate to paint the walls with your brains."

From behind Lava, Ricky's eyebrows shot upward. He bent his head to untie Sal's knots.

"I see movement!" Sal said from the window. "There's someone in the trees across the road."

Ricky ran to the window, leaving Lava tied. Tom repositioned himself to he could look toward the windows, but still keep his gun trained on Lava.

The rapport of rifle shot rang out.

"My God," Ricky said. "Laurel's head just exploded."

"Get down!" Sal shouted. He dove for the floor, his bulk sending an end table sliding across the floor. Ricky and Tom flattened on the floor as the front windows imploded, scattering shards of glass all over the living room.

Lava shouted, "Get me out of here!"

Dozens of bullet-holes pockmarked the front of the house, sending splinters flying as starry pockets of light shone through the holes.

"Is it Huks?" Tom shouted over the din.

"I can't see who shot Laurel," Sal said. The shooting stopped, and Ricky rose to his hands and knees, crawled toward the side of Lava's couch, pushed it toward the center of the floor as a barrier between the men and the outside shooters.

Tom glanced around. No sense barricading the door; there was little of it left. He and Sal quickly knelt behind the sofa.

Sal looked at Tom. "I don't think it's Huks."

Tom rose on his knees and grabbed Lava by the collar, turning over the chair and dragging both man and chair behind the couch barrier. Tom shoved his face within an inch of Lava's. "Who did this? Who is watching you? Who shot Laurel?"

"How should I know!"

Tom shook the man so violently that Lava's head bounced against the floor. "You know! Who shot Laurel?"

Lava tried to spit on Tom, but instead the spit dribbled off his chin and landed on his barong.

Disgusted, Tom grunted and shoved Lava away.

The door burst inward and bits of material and stuffing flew through the air as fresh shots erupted. Ricky rose up to fire back, but a rifle butt cracked the side of his head. His eyes rolled skyward as he fell stiffly to the floor like a falling tree.

Sal fired three rounds, dropping two men who wore bandanas over their faces.

In the ruckus, Tom never heard the four men who came up behind him. One kicked Sal in the head, sending him sprawling across the floor where his head connected with the wooden desk, knocking him cold.

Tom felt himself being lifted off the ground. He struggled, but two men gripped his arms, dragged him backward and out the door. He saw the back of a fourth man as he lifted Lava, chair and all, hoisting him into the air, and then all went dark as damp, rough burlap was wound around Tom's face.

Chapter 39

IT WAS TOO difficult for Tom to determine how far they'd ridden in the back of the dark truck. He knew the road was rutted and rocky, but time played tricks on him as seconds seemed to stretch into minutes, minutes into hours. The truck they rode in stank of hay. No, that could be the burlap covering his face. He listened to the murmur of voices, but he couldn't make out the words or even the language the men spoke over the groaning of the truck's loud engine, the creaking of its axles and joints as it rocked side-to-side over the bumpy, furrowed road. He turned his head, angling his ear toward the side panel of the truck as he heard screeching metal.

Trees. They were heading deep into the jungle.

Beside him, Lava continued to talk.

"Shut up!" Tom said. "I can't hear. We need to listen. See if you can make out what they're saying."

Lava's talking persisted. "We are both going to die, FBI man. Let's see who is the tough guy now!"

Tom worked his hands behind his back, trying to loosen the hemp with which he was bound. Movement caused the rope to cut into his stinging wrists, and within moments, he felt blood on his palms and knew he was doing more damage than good with his now-swollen, clumsy fingers.

What seemed like an hour later, but could have been only fifteen or twenty minutes, the truck lurched to a squeaking stop. The voices grew louder, and Tom now recognized the language as Tagalog. *Hukbalahap!* It wasn't Yakuza, after all.

So why had they kidnapped one of their own? Why was Lava bound and thrown into the truck beside of him?

Tom wouldn't get answers anytime soon, because as he was dragged out of the truck, he took a blow to the head that caused the world to again go black around him.

Sometime later, he revived enough to realize he sat tied to a chair. He struggled to open his eyes, but they were heavy-lidded. At least the burlap wound around his face had been removed. His head pounded, and the light from the bare bulb hanging overhead seared his brain. What a great time for a migraine. Tom's stomach lurched, but he swallowed his gorge.

He heard shuffling and forced open his eyes enough to realize two Huks armed with rifles stood against the wall in front of him, several feet apart. He squinted and glanced to each side. Lava sat beside him, still tied to the chair from his house, though he, too wore no face cover. The man's face was cut and bloodied. Tom suspected his own looked the same. He closed his eyes, willing the blinding pain behind them to subside.

Tom must have faded out again, or slept for unknown hours as he often did when a migraine took hold of him, because when he roused again, the light above him had been turned out, and what appeared to be clear light of morning came through the high windows in the barn-like building where he was held hostage. Two Huks still guarded them, but they were different men. A changing of the guard. Lava snored softly in the chair beside of him. Tom's cut lips burned when he smiled in spite of the dire situation.

His headache had subsided, though a dull ache persisted in the back of his head. The memory of the blow he'd taken resurfaced, and he wondered how hard he'd been hit. He ran through the laundry list of events that had taken place since he'd last had a good morning, before they'd met with Santos and his men. His brain seemed to be working fine. One good thing, at least.

Tom's neck creaked as he turned his head to look around him. His entire body ached, and when he tried to move, he realized not only were his hands still tied behind his back, but his ankles were tied to the chair legs, and his arms had been stretched over the back of the chair, causing his shoulders to feel like they'd been pulled out of their sockets. One of the Huks looked up then, stood straighter, looked alert. Footsteps sounded from Tom's left, and he turned stiffly to see Father Diaz approach. The man wore his cassock, the large gold cross swinging from a thick chain around his neck. He clasped his hands passively in front of him as he walked toward Tom and stood in front of him.

"I didn't ask for absolution, *Father*. I am placing you under arrest." Tom said.

One of the guards stepped forward, his rifle raised in the air with the butt of it aimed at Tom's head. Santa Romana lifted his hand to stay the man.

Beside of Tom, Lava looked at Santa Romana and whimpered, "Did my information check out?"

Great. You're awake *now*. Tom turned his head and shot the worthless man a scathing look.

Lava coughed, and his words came out on a snivel. "Father! Please, Father, bless me. Bless me, Father, for I have told you the truth about the gold."

Santa Romana turned, a beatific smile on his face. He made the sign of the cross, then stepped toward Lava, bent forward and kissed the man's forehead. Lava broke into a deep, heaving sob.

"Untie this man," Santa Romana said. "We have unfinished business that I will attend to myself. Your information was correct."

Tom sneered at the man. "For Christ's sake, you tie the man up, beat the hell of him, then you give him a blessing?"

Santa Romana turned toward Tom, giving him a sorrowful look. "He is not your concern. You will come with me, Thomas Warren." He continued to stare at Tom, placidly now, as one of the Huk guards hustled forward and knelt to untie Tom's ankles. "Keep his hands tied behind his back. I expect he will not be docile."

Thirty minutes later, Tom bumped back down the rutted road out of the jungle, but this time he sat in the passenger seat of Santa Romana's sedan. He looked out the window, but recognized nothing; no house, dilapidated barn, road sign or other distinguishing landmark existed in the dense jungle.

"You didn't blindfold me," Tom said dryly. "Does that mean you're going to kill me?"

"I am a priest," Santa Romana said. "It is a commandment of God that I shall not kill." He hunched his tall frame over the steering wheel and looked at Tom. Besides, I trust that you will be gone before *too* long."

"Trust," Tom muttered. *Trust no one. Not even a man of God.* Lieutenant Colonel Santos's words came back to him. Had the man known Santa Romana would kidnap him? Had it all been an orchestrated set-up? Tom couldn't believe that was true. Santos wanted to squash the Huks, perhaps even more than Tom.

"I have questions for you, Thomas Warren."

Tom snorted. "So? I have questions of my own I'd like answered."

"That is fair," Santa Romana said. "You, first. Answer one of my questions, then I will answer one of yours."

"Why should I believe you?"

Santa Romana looked at Tom, his stare incredulous. "Because I do *not* lie. To anyone."

Tom's tongue sought out his busted lip, and he winced at the pain and taste of dried blood. He turned and glared at Santa Romana. "I know you're digging the stolen war loot. Getting rich. Obviously, your front is that of a Catholic priest, in order to work with your Huks. A priest who keeps spirits at bay. But I'm not afraid of ghosts."

Santa Romana glanced at Tom, then looked at the road and glanced back at Tom again. "I *am* a priest, but I am not taking *anything*. You are mistaken, Mr. Warren." He frowned, and his smooth forehead furrowed into shiny rows. "Am I protecting the place where I believe gold is buried? Yes, I am. You see, I, too, was interviewing Mr. Lava. I verified his information. But this effort is not for my own wealth or well-being. This gold, this *particular* burial site, belongs to a very good friend of mine. An American." He fixed Tom in an earnest stare.

An American? Did he mean Lansdale?

"The man to whom the gold belongs gave his life for our country spying on the Japanese." Santa Romana pursed his lips and breathed heavily through his nose. "He died protecting many people. He fathered a son a few years before his tragic end, and when his son is old enough, he will return for it." Santa Romana stared out the windshield, but it seemed it wasn't the rough and rutted road he saw before him. "It is my duty to protect the gold, for when the man's heir returns to claim it."

"Your duty." Tom found that hard to believe.

"Yes, my duty. Besides . . ." Santa Romana sniffed. "Those burial sites are unsafe. They are booby-trapped. Mines collapse. There are traps. No one should dig on that mountain. Many men have died trying to recover gold at various sites all over the Philippines, but especially on Montalban Gorge. Men like your FBI friend." He shrugged. "I have nothing to do with that."

Tom spoke through clenched teeth. "It hasn't kept you from recovering gold. Besides my friend did not die digging for buried treasure. My friend was murdered—*beaten* and murdered, tortured, by the damned Japanese Yakuza." He turned his face toward the window, stewing.

The passing scenery caught his attention. They were now in familiar territory. He'd been so caught up in conversation that he hadn't paid attention to the way they'd come. Tom relaxed a bit when Santa Romana turned toward downtown Manila. He likely wouldn't kill him in public, despite what Sal and Ricky thought.

Sal and Ricky. Where were they? Had they been captured, too? Were they looking for him? Were they . . . were they dead?

Tom pushed away the thought. He turned toward Santa Romana. "Look, *Father*, I know you're dealing with Dr. Wang. But what you may not know is that Wang is not just a banker; he's also a Communist agent."

The muscle in Santa Romana's jaw twitched. "Shut up, Warren."

"Touch a nerve, did I? I'll bet I know a few other things about your banker-buddy that you don't know. Like he has a fondness for chopsticks."

Santa Romana slammed the brakes, throwing Tom forward so that his head thumped hard against the dashboard. He then drove onward. "I said *shut up*." Venom filled his voice. "You think you know things . . . important things. You know just enough to get yourself killed, Mr. Warren, and I don't want to see any more Americans die on my watch."

Any more Americans . . . It didn't sound to Tom like the man was talking only about his late friend. Had he seen Snake die, too?

"I want you out of my country now, Mr. Warren. To stay here will surely cost you your life."

Tom shook his head. "No. I cannot leave. Not now. I have a mission to complete for the FBI, and I can't leave until it is finished." Santa Romana couldn't want him out any more desperately than Tom wanted out himself. Or could he? "Look, Santa Romana, if you want me out of the Philippines, help me out. Believe me, I want out of here, but I can't leave until the Hukbalahap Rebellion is put to an end. The FBI will not release me or allow me to leave until then."

Tom realized they'd turned onto the street leading past the FBI building . . . an area Santa Romana obviously knew well. Now Tom was surprised to hear the man chuckle, though his laugh was anything but good-humored.

"Mr. Warren, the FBI is the least of my worries. The FBI no longer has any authority in the Philippines. Do yourself a favor. Pack your bags and get out." Santa Romana reached across Tom and pulled the door handle, opening the passenger door. He lifted a foot and simultaneously shoved and kicked Tom out onto the street, then stomped the accelerator and drove away as horns blared around them.

Chapter 40

Manilla, Philippines
September 18, 1952

FATHER JOSE ANTONIO Diaz, known by a select few by his birth name of Jose Garcia Santa Romana, walked into the church's candlelit vestibule and crossed himself as he gazed at the massive wooden cross at the front of the sanctuary. He slipped into his sacristy, where he removed his cassock and hung it on the wooden frame behind the door. Tenderly, he breathed a heartfelt prayer, then kissed the heavy cross that hung around his neck—a cross that had been blessed by the Pope.

Santa Romana felt like himself again, and he smiled. He knelt on the floor, but not to pray. Instead, he pushed aside the heavy, hand-woven rug and revealed the secret door in the floor. He lifted the hatch, pleased to see soft light shine forth. He lifted his muscled frame into the hole, his feet finding purchase on the smooth wooden rungs of the ladder he'd installed decades ago, when they'd first built the underground passageway. He stepped down into the large, clean tunnel and followed it to the small bungalow far behind the church. He retrieved the golden skeleton key from the cord around his waist and unlocked the heavily waxed wooden door. The small, neat office glowed with warm light, and Edward Lansdale looked up from the book he was reading. He sat with his legs comfortably crossed on the one of the two antique leather chairs that sat across from Santa Romana's intricately carved Italian desk.

"Have you been waiting long?" asked Santa Romana.

"Not at all." Lansdale held up his snifter in salute. "Actually, I enjoy spending time down here. It's a pleasure to settle in with a good book and a snifter of warm brandy in your little cocoon, Santy."

Santa Romana's smile felt tight. "I'm glad you enjoy it."

Lansdale studied him for a moment. "You didn't invite me here for the ambiance, however."

"No, I did not." Santa Romana settled into the high-backed chair behind his desk, reached for the bottle of brandy he kept on the corner and splashed some into a glass. "We must shut down our operation for a while. Immediately." He swirled the amber liquid around the glass, then took a long sip, felt his throat and chest warm as it slid down. "Your FBI man Warren . . . he knows too much."

Lansdale's face paled, and his eyebrows knit into a severe line. "I see."

"I want you to get me out of the country until this blows over."

Lansdale nodded. "We'll work something out. I'll make a few calls."

Santa Romana leaned forward, his muscled frame seeming to grow in the small room. "Now. I want out *now.*"

Lansdale quickly sat down the snifter, uncrossed his legs and scooted forward on the chair. "I see. Okay. Okay." His eyes grew round behind his eyeglasses. "I'll get Nguyen Tao to come. He's in Vietnam right now, on assignment for me, but don't worry. I know MacArthur will not question your desire, or even your reason for leaving the Philippines. You have our full support." He smiled again, but this time his smile was eager. No one in his right mind wanted to rile Santa Romana, and the US government needed him. Desperately. Lansdale and Santa Romana continued to share their bottle of aged brandy. Finally, Lansdale said, "If you are leaving, I assume you are finished with the Huks?"

"Yes. Until General Santos and President Magasaysay are finished with their campaign against them, I can no longer discreetly recover gold."

Lansdale drew a deep breath and held up his glass. Santa Romana tapped it with his, and they both finished the sniffers of brandy.

"You know, if you want more time, I can get it for you," Lansdale said.

"No, too much attention has been drawn to our operation. The gold will be here waiting for us." Santa Romana sat for a moment, jutted his jaw and said, "Besides, I have some banking to fix. How soon can you get Tao here?" Santa Romana leaned forward another inch. Lansdale was afraid of him, he knew. He could destroy the man with one phone call.

"I'll make certain he flies out tomorrow. He will be here in the afternoon, We'll have him land on the abandoned runway at Baguio, Camp John Hay. It's not a very long flight, but he'll be here by tomorrow night."

Santa Romana nodded. "Tomorrow afternoon. So be it."

Chapter 41

Montalban Gorge, Philippines
September 19, 1952

THE WIND WHIPPED Santa Romana's barong tagalong around his muscled torso as he stood beside Congressman Ferdinand Marcos on the sandy crest at Montalban Gorge. The fog lifted from the valley below and rose closer to where they now stood.

Santa Romana watched the man from the corner of his eye. Marcos had served as his attorney for several years, yet Santa Romana still refused to relinquish complete trust to the man. Marcos was too power-hungry. "Wealth is power," Marcos had once told him, and Santy knew the man believed that above all else and would stop at nothing to reach his goal—to become the richest man in the world.

A satisfied, confident smile crept across Santa Romana's lips. Having knowledge of a man's deepest motivation gave one more power than wealth ever could.

He clapped a hand on Marcos's back. "Sorry for the early morning meeting. This is where we will begin, Congressman. I must leave for a short time." Marcos's back broadened beneath Santa Romana's hand.

"One day, Santy," Marcos said, puffing out his chest. "One day, I will be president."

Santa Romana had expected this declaration for a long time, but it still caused his eyebrows to rise. "Do you believe that, Marcos?"

The man jutted out his chin and pursed his lips. "Of course I believe it." He turned slowly, looking out over the mountainside, then out over the gorge. "We will make our own rules, Santy. When I become President of the Philippines,

I will rule with a firm, yet benevolent hand." He turned and looked at Santa Romana. "You will be by my side, Jose Garcia Santa Romana. You and I will be praised throughout the islands. The Communists will cease to exist. The world will honor us for saving the Philippines and rebuilding this country as a democracy."

Santa Romana stared out, watching as fog curled over the ground where they now stood, eddying around his feet. Soon the drive off the twisting mountain would be difficult to make in the thickening fog. He looked at Ferdinand Marcos, studied the man for a moment. "I will be happy to support you in your rise to the presidency, Ferdinand." He paused, watching the man intently. "But I have no desire for the public's attention. I prefer to remain unseen. In the background, so I can finish my work and my mission."

Marcos chuckled. "A ghost. You want to remain a ghost. It is hard to be a ghost when the entire country wants to laud your accomplishments, Santy." He smiled indulgently. "And believe me, there is much we shall accomplish together."

Santa Romana reached into the neckline of his barong tagalong and pulled out his gold cross, kissed it, then tucked it back inside the shirt. "The honor and glory can be all yours, my friend."

"Ahhh, trust me, Santy. You will want all the power and recognition you deserve, once I am President of the Philippines."

Another breeze lifted the fog, and it now grew thicker around them. Santa Romana shook his head as his friend continued to talk of his lofty aspirations. Tired of the boasting, he turned and walked away from the outcrop.

"I've said it before," Marcos continued. "Wealth is power."

Santa Romana shook his head as he ducked alone among the low-hanging branches on the path leading down to where he'd parked his car. "Fool," he muttered. "*Knowledge* is power."

Congressman Marcos spread his arms wide. "Yes, Santy, you will be proud to stand alongside me one day."

Santa Romana shook his head, took a step backwards, and silently walked away.

Chapter 42

Guillermo Capadocia's hideout - Pantay, Philippines
September 19, 1952

TOM PATTED THE pocket of his flak jacket, checking once again for extra ammunition. His heart beat in his ears, too loud and too fast. When he signed up as a special agent in FBI intelligence, he thought he'd love the exotic travel, the intrigue of investigation and the opportunity to put his extensive foreign language prowess to use. And it was true; he did. But he hadn't counted on being—quite literally—in the line of fire, walking a too-fine wire between life and death.

A twig snapped beside of Tom, and his heart lurched. "Damn it, Sal," he whispered as fiercely as he dared. "You scared me half to death."

Sal grinned. "Sorry," he mouthed. He pointed a thick finger over Tom's shoulder. "Santos and his men are in place. He said we should follow his lead when they attack."

Tom turned as Ricky approached, his body hunkered low to the ground. The man's stealth was amazing; Tom never heard him coming. When all three were gathered behind the stand of palmettos fifty or so yards away from Guillermo Capadocia's hideout, Tom gave direction in low whispers. "If you have to shoot, shoot to kill. We've been battered by the Huks and Yakuza enough, and they're playing for keeps. We have no reason to take hostages. Protect yourselves as we protect each other. It is finished here and now." He pointed with two fingers to his left. "Sal, you go that way. Get as close to the building as you can, without being seen." He looked at Ricky. "You take the right. Circle around to the other side; come up on the far side of the building. Their vehicles should offer cover. I'll take the middle. We'll have their only exit and their vehicles covered."

Both men nodded and quietly slunk away. The utter quiet unnerved Tom. Even the birds had grown silent. Within minutes, Sal signaled that he'd found a vantage point. A moment later, Ricky did the same.

Now they waited. Waited for Santos to make his move.

Tom worked to measure his breathing in an effort to slow his galloping heart. His gut told him this was it—the beginning of the end. Capadocia lurked inside that building, and any time now, he'd have to come out. When he did, they'd take him, and Tom's mission would be over.

He could go home.

Unbidden, images of Judy and Izzy rose in his mind. He'd already wasted much of his young adult life here in the Philippines, and he had nothing to show for it but fresh wariness and scars. Life in the US would never feel the same, but it still had to be better than this.

Movement caught his eye. The building's only door opened ahead of him, but only by a few inches. Enough that whomever stood on the other side could peer out. Tom realized he was holding his breath, and he exhaled a slow, steady stream of air through pursed lips.

A few seconds later, the door swung open. Out walked a man in a gray suit. Dr. Wang!

Tom pointed at Sal, then toward the front door. Sal lifted his gun and took aim. Oh, no! Tom waved as frantically as he dared. Sal misunderstood. He was going to—

Before Tom could get Sal's attention, the sound of a shot exploded the quiet atmosphere. Dr. Wang broke into a run. Unbelievably, Sal's bullet had missed him!

Suddenly gunshots erupted all around Capadocia's compound. Tom jerked his head from side to side, unsure who shot and from where. He saw the uniform of one of Santos's men move in the bushes across the packed-down grassy area where vehicles were parked. Then he saw another.

Tom's pulse raced and he panted for breath. He gripped his .38 revolver, unsure of where to turn. *Wang!* Where was Dr. Wang? Then he saw the man dive toward a sedan. He raised his revolver to shoot when a noise beside of him caused him to whirl about. "Sal!" Tom hissed. He sucked in a breath. "I could have shot you!"

Sal crouched beside Tom, pointed a finger toward the same side of the building he'd just left. Ricky's head emerged behind a shrub. Tom motioned, and Ricky crept low to the ground, moving faster toward him than Tom would have believed possible in that position. The gunfire ceased, and the tense air grew eerily quiet.

Tom moved into position to shoot Wang, who crept on his belly between some of the dozen vehicles. Sal touched Tom's arm, then pointed to the front door of the building. It opened again, this time about a foot. Someone flung the door all the way open and darted out, running pell-mell toward a Jeep that sat off to itself. Guillermo Capadocia! Tom swung his revolver, but before he could pull the trigger, a shotgun blast sounded, and Capadocia was lifted a couple of feet of the ground as he flew backward. Dirt puffed from between blades of grass as his body landed heavily on the ground. "Santos's men got Capadocia!" Ricky whispered as he knelt at Tom's side.

A tingling thrill raced through Tom's body, filling him with renewed vigor. "We've got to get Wang."

As he spoke the words, one of the last sedans in the row fired to life and spun out of the field, heading straight toward the dirt road. Tom, Sal and Ricky pointed guns in tandem, but there was no need to fire, as guns went off from the other direction, zinging bullets off Wang's car.

"Get down!" Tom ordered. He turned, talking as he crawled out of the palmetto stand. "Let's get back to the car. We've got catch Wang."

Chapter 43

Santo Tomas, Philippines
September 19, 1952

TOM GRIPPED THE back of the front seat as Sal swung the car sideways, blocking the dock entrance to the water just before the clearing at Lingayen Gulf. They saw Dr. Wang's car ahead of them, and just to the right, a small shack at the water's edge. But no Dr. Wang.

A small boat pulled up to the dock. Dr. Wang jumped out of the shack. Ricky, Sal and Tom flung open their car doors, squatting behind them, guns drawn and pointed toward Dr. Wang, who ran headlong down the dock toward the awaiting boat.

Ricky fired, and dock-boards splintered at Wang's feet. Sal sprang out from behind the car door and ran. A barrage of bullets erupted from the small shack at water's edge. He raised his weapon and fired, fired again. Then click. He turned and raced toward Tom.

They retreated into the tree line behind them. Tom reached into his pocket for an extra box of ammo to throw toward Sal. He opened the box and took out six bullets for himself, then closed up the rest in the box. He turned to throw the box, then realized Sal was gone. He saw movement in his periphery and turned in time to see Sal tackle a man who'd aimed a rifle at Tom. The rifle discharged as Sal flattened the man.

Ricky fired again toward the boat. Bullets began to rain like hailstones into the trees as several Hukbalahap guerillas returned fire. Quickly, they moved farther up into the foliage of the jungle for cover.

Tom watched in despair as Dr. Wang pulled away from the dock in a small motor boat. There was *nothing* he could do about it.

Gunfire erupted from behind him. They were surrounded. "We gotta get out of here!" Tom shouted. "We're trapped."

Ricky ran to Tom. "Where's Sal?" he panted.

"He was right behind me." Tom pointed to where Sal had tackled the shooter. "I'll go get him. You get the car. Drive it up the road, past the bend. We'll exit the jungle and meet you there."

"Gotcha!" Ricky ran zig-zagged back through the jungle.

Tom darted from tree to tree, watching for Sal. Bullets continued to rain around him. He restrained from returning fire—he needed to save his bullets for clear shots.

But where was Sal? Tom swiped brush out of his way. There, in front of him, was the man Sal had tackled—and Sal still lay on top of him. Confusion clouded Tom's brain. Why hadn't Sal gotten up? Surely the shooter was dead.

Tom reached his compatriot and rolled Sal off the dead Huk. Sal had fatally stabbed the man. "Sal," Tom said. "Get up. Hurry."

Sal didn't respond.

Tom fell to his knees next to him. "Sal!" He smacked Sal's cheeks, still with no response. Sal's shirt was crimson with the Huk's blood. Or so he thought. "Dear God." Tom lifted Sal's bulky torso onto his lap. "Sal!"

Sal's eyes fluttered opened. "Tom." The word strangled in his throat and he coughed, spraying a fine mist of blood onto Tom's khaki jacket. He closed his eyes.

Tom's vision blurred, and he gently shook Sal as he pulled him toward his chest. "Sal!" A bullet whizzed past Tom's ear. Quickly, gun drawn, he hunkered down and look around for who had shot at them.

Sal's eyes opened again, but they appeared dim. "I did my job." His eyes closed.

Tom bent his face to Sal's. No breath. His friend was gone.

Tom looked at the car moving toward the bend of the road.

Ricky jumped out of the car, his .38 Special in the air. He aimed toward Tom, and the bullet whistled past Tom's ear. A Huk fell from behind him. Ricky whistled and frantically waved for Tom to hurry. He flipped around and shot in the opposite direction.

A rifle blasted from the road. The back of Ricky's head exploded. He was dead before he hit the ground.

A strangled cry reached Tom's ears before he realized it was his own. A sudden surge of rage coursed through his veins. For a moment, he expected his own head to explode. He grabbed the dead Huk's rifle and opened fire, shooting at anything that moved.

When the rifle had spent its bullets, Tom flung it to the ground and reached for his .38 revolver. He sensed someone behind him and whirled around, the pistol pointed. "Santa Romana!"

His world flashed blue, then blackness consumed him.

Chapter 44

Capadocia's hideout - Pantay, Philippines
September 19, 1952

TOM'S NECK AND face hurt. His jaw felt like it had been sewn shut, and when he tried to open his mouth, he winced in pain.

"He's awake!" said a thickly accented man's voice. "You!"

Tom looked up to see a tall, thin, Huk guerilla with a navy blue bandana around his neck. He held a rifle by the barrel in one hand, and waved his other hand in the air as he spoke. "You killed Guillermo Capadocia," the man said in a chilling tone.

Tom tried to move, but he was again strapped to a chair. He wriggled his hands, and though his wrists still bore the healing cuts from the rope he'd last been tied with, this time it felt different. He stroked his fingers along the binding. Cotton strips. Strange. But still, here he was again, in a hostage situation. *Great.* If he lived through this one, he was on the next plane to the US, come hell, high water, or Hoover. The FBI be damned. He opened his mouth to speak, and again stiffness and pain in his jaw caused him to yelp.

"It will be sore for a while." Santa Romana walked toward Tom, his spotless cassock swaying side-to-side as he stepped. "I'm afraid your jaw dislocated. Not to worry. While you were out, I popped it back into place." His face remained serene.

What had happened before this? Tom's aching head refused to think. Images popped up. Unwanted images. Sal's last words as he covered the Huk. He'd taken a bullet for Tom.

Vomit churned in Tom's stomach. Ricky? He, too, had given his life for Tom. Tom shuddered, then carefully opened and closed his mouth, unwelcome tears springing to his eyes as he worked the swollen muscles. His head throbbed, and another wave of nausea washed over him. "You did it." His voice came out thick and dry. He yearned for a drink of water.

Santa Romana offered a slight shrug. "You were uncooperative."

The Huk rushed forward. "You killed Capadocia!" He rammed the butt of his rifle into Tom's unprotected stomach.

Tom lurched to the side and vomited, his jaw popping loudly as he opened it to throw up, but it was only a dry heave. He spat several times, keeping his head turned to the side. When he finally looked up, Santa Romana held a cup of water and a cloth. When had the man gotten them? Tom hadn't seen him move. He glanced around, but the guerilla Huk still stood near the door, still glaring at him. There was no way he'd imagined the punch to the gut. But. . . .

"Drink," Santa Romana said.

Tom swished the first mouthful of water around his mouth and spat it on the ground. Then he gulped long sips, as Santa Romana patiently held the cup to his lips, then wiped his mouth. "Untie me," Tom said.

"In time."

Tom shut his eyes against the pounding in his head, and when he opened them, the Huk stood beside Santa Romana, viciously glaring at Tom.

"Let me have him," the Huk said.

Santa Romana did not move, but spoke in an even voice to the Huk. "Leave me alone with him. I will find out the truth."

A vile laugh escaped the Huk's mouth, and he leaned toward Tom. "You will be sorry now, Mister FBI. He will do to you what he did to Yamashita's driver, Kashii." He laughed again, throwing back his head. "You will wish it was me who had killed you!" The Huk continued laughing as he left the room, but Santa Romana's taciturn expression still did not change.

Somewhere behind Tom, a door slammed shut as the Huk left the room. Tom looked up at Santa Romana.

"More water?" Santa Romana asked.

Tom shook his head. Who was this man? How could he switch from beating and tying him up to caring for his well-being? How could he change from guerilla to priest? No wonder some of the Filipinos feared the man they believed commanded spirits.

Santa Romana walked up to Tom, looked at him with an expression that could only be described as part sadness, part relief. "It is over."

The pounding in Tom's head replaced itself with a dull ache behind his eyes. He desperately wanted sleep. He forced himself to look at the man, though it pained him to focus. "Nothing is over. You let Dr. Wang get away." Tom curled his lips into a sneer. "Don't you know he's after the gold you're claim to protect? You're a fool."

Santa Romana shook his head. "If you believe that Dr. Wang is a free man, you are the fool, Mr. Warren." He stared at Tom for a full minute, then he pressed his lips together.

"So," said Tom, "you're going to kill him? You? A priest? You're going to kill the man who is after your gold?" Tom forced a sarcastic, raspy laugh.

Santa Romana stared at Tom. "I will never touch him." He clasped his hands together piously.

"What? You'll command one of your Huk minions to kill him?"

"I would never tell one man to take the life of another." He tilted his head to one side. "Information is a powerful thing, however. It can cause people to react in surprising ways." Santa Romana briefly closed his eyes, smiled, then opened them. "Pay attention, Agent Warren." He looked over Tom's shoulder toward the door as he pulled out the heavy gold cross he wore around his neck, kissed it, then slipped it back inside his cassock. "Edgardo!"

The door creaked open, and the guerilla Huk marched toward Santa Romana, his eyes gleaming. "At your service." He looked at Tom, and his eyebrows lifted a bit, as if surprised to see Tom still intact.

Santa Romana turned and faced the Huk. "I have found out who killed Guillermo Capadocia." His expression grew grim. "It was Dr. Wang."

Edgardo's face grew red, then almost purple as color crept up his neck. He thrust his rifle into the air. "We will kill him! Dr. Wang is a dead man!" Edgardo turned and jogged from the room, pumping his rifle in the air. "Dr. Wang is a dead man!"

The door slammed again and Santa Romana slowly turned his entire body to face Tom. He folded his hands behind his back as Edgardo's continued cheer faded into distance. Santa Romana stared at Tom. "That, Mr. Warren, is how it is done. Information changes things. Knowledge is power."

Tom swallowed. "What now? What happens to me?"

Santa Romana offered a pleasant smile. "Now you go to see your friend."

Friend? Friends? His dead friends?

"Edward Lansdale. He is waiting for you at Camp John Hay. General MacArthur arranged a plane for you."

Tom's sore jaw dropped open. "MacArthur?" He stared at this man, this priest, this spirit-tamer who pulled strings like a puppeteer. "Who *are* you?"

Santa Romana smiled again, a gentle, prideless smile, but said nothing.

"You have no control over me. I have a mission to complete, and you're crazy if you think Lansdale and MacArthur are waiting with a plane for me." Anger surged through Tom's chest and he struggled to free himself. "You say you are a priest, yet you're in cahoots with the Philippine military, the US military, the FBI . . . hell, even the Pope!"

Tom wriggled his hands against the cotton strips binding them, but the strips failed to loosen. If he could only get his hands free, this insane priest-man was going down.

Santa Romana grabbed Tom's jacket collar and pulled him so close that Tom could smell the bitter coffee on the man's breath. "You have no idea who I am," Santa Romana said through clenched teeth. He roughly shoved Tom, nearly toppling him and the chair. "In your world, I do not exist."

Santa Romana stepped behind Tom, and Tom held his breath, sure that a blow was soon to follow. Instead, the strap binding Tom to the chair grew tighter, then fell away. The man had untied him from the chair, but his hands were still bound.

Tom took the first deep breath he'd had in hours. He filled his lungs with air so quickly he became lightheaded. Strong hands gripped his upper arms, and he felt himself being lifted from behind off the chair. A throb pulsed behind his eyes at the minor change in altitude, and he staggered on his feet. The hands held him until he regained his sense of balance.

Santa Romana stepped in front of him, then took him by the arm, gently, yet insistently, guiding him toward the door that led out of the stark, concrete room. "Do not speak until we are in the car," he said, his voice low and adamant.

When Santa Romana opened the door, Tom blinked in surprise. The room they entered was neatly furnished with modern furniture in bright colors. Tapestries hung on the walls, and though there were no windows, the white-painted walls gave the room an air of openness. *Capadocia's hideout.* How Tom guessed this was where he was being held, he wasn't sure, but he realized Guillermo Capadocia hadn't exactly been living in a hostage's squalor. The scent of sweet tobacco and strong coffee filled the air, and Tom's mouth watered for a taste of either.

"Do not make eye contact with anyone," Santa Romana whispered. "Look straight ahead."

Tom did as instructed, allowing Santa Romana to march him through the large room where at least seven men sat in various groupings, talking among themselves. They grew quiet as Tom and Santa Romana walked through, yet no one addressed them.

Outside, Tom squinted against the overcast daylight. He looked around, recognized that indeed he'd been held at Capadocia's hideout. Heavy clouds hung low like massive gray stones. The air felt moist and cool against his burning face, and he drank deep gulps of the mountain breeze. Santa Romana shoved Tom into the sedan too soon. "Can you roll down the window?" Tom asked. "I don't want to get sick again. I need fresh air."

Santa Romana's smooth brow furrowed, but he rolled down the passenger window a few inches. They drove down the mountain road and turned onto the deeply rutted road Tom remembered from before. Despite the condition of the bumpy road, Santa Romana drove at a reckless speed, though he turned the steering wheel deftly left and right, navigating the terrain with complete familiarity. He'd obviously been there often.

"So you're directing the Communist Huks," Tom said. "Or what's left of them."

Santa Romana scowled. "You will never learn, will you? What you think you know is only enough to get you killed." Then Santa Romana leaned closer to Warren. "Your mission is finished. The Huks are done. I have finished them for you!"

"You've kidnapped me *twice*. I'm a United States federal agent. If what you say is true, and I'm really heading back to the US, then when I get there and tell Hoover the truth about what you're up to, you can bet you'll go down."

A bitter smile curved Santa Romana's lips. "You are a fool, Thomas Warren." He shook his head in amazement. "An utter fool."

Tom leaned the side of his head against the cool window glass, tilted up his face, drank in the damp air. "Lansdale may think he knows you, but he has no idea how corrupt you really are." Tom closed his eyes. *But that's about to change.*

Chapter 45

Camp John Hay Air Station, Baguio City, Philippines
September 19, 1952

WIND RUFFLED THROUGH thigh-high grass that grew unhampered on both sides of the abandoned runway at Camp John Hay. Dark clouds formed a backdrop, rolling closer with each wind gust. A large airplane waited at the end of the runway, the low roar of its engines growing louder and mixing with distant thunder as they drew near.

Santa Romana was telling the truth! Tom's stomach fluttered—not unpleasantly— as he realized he'd soon be back home in America. A strange thrill raced through his entire body, and he shivered. First things first. He'd shower and have a big meal. Steak and lobster! Then he'd call Willoughby. No, he couldn't trust Willoughby. He had to figure out the best way to address Hoover, how to delicately present the news about Lansdale and Santa Romana's covert operation, how to break it to the President of the United States that he'd been a cheap pawn in a very ugly game where the chess pieces were bank accounts stuffed with gold.

Santa Romana drove the sedan past the governor's mansion, onto the airfield, and right up to the airplane. A small, concrete building stood thirty yards from the plane. A man dressed in a gray flannel suit stepped out of the building. *Dr. Wang!* Tom sucked in his breath. No. It wasn't Dr. Wang. It was Edward Lansdale. And beside him walked a compact, thin Vietnamese man dressed in a khaki pants and a blue knit shirt with dual breast-pockets— distinctively American attire. He had seen that man before with Santa Romana in Hong Kong.

Santa Romana stopped the car and looked at Tom. "You can get out now."

Right. His hands were still tied behind his back.

Santa Romana grinned. *Grinned!*

Tom clenched his teeth. The man was toying with him. Perhaps a final parting shot. Tom could hardly wait to take him down. Santa Romana stepped out of the car, his cassock flapping. He walked around and opened the passenger door, then grasped Tom's arm and assisted him out of the car.

Lansdale walked toward them, one hand holding his hat to his head against the wind. "For God's sake, untie him!"

Santa Romana did as Lansdale said.

Lansdale looked at Tom, his expression severe. "Warren, this is Nguyen Tao. Tao will be your liaison in Saigon."

"Saigon!" Tom looked at Santa Romana, then at the man called Tao, then at Lansdale. He rubbed his aching wrists as he turned back to Santa Romana. "You said I was going to the US!"

Santa Romana nodded toward Lansdale.

"You will," Lansdale said, "but not yet. You need to fully recover first."

"Recover?" A chill of dread raced across Tom's scalp. He rolled stiff shoulders. "I'm fine. Headache is all." He glared at Santa Romana.

Tao reached into his front pants pocket, pulled out a small leather case, and unzipped it. He held up a vial and syringe in one hand, then nodded solemnly at Santa Romana.

"Is that what I think it is?" Lansdale asked.

"Yes. Two-hundred-fifty micrograms of LSD---Lysergic acid diethylamide. It's a real mind eraser." Tao slid the leather case back into his pocket, then inserted the needle into the vial and pulled back on the metal rings, drawing liquid into the syringe. "It's still in the experimental stages, but it's worked well on several subjects thus far."

Santa Romana smiled and looked from Lansdale to Tom. "What better time to give it another trial?"

Tom stiffened. "No, not that?"

Lansdale and Santa Romana each grabbed one of Tom's arms. He struggled against the men. Tom pulled the Lansdale arm loose and slammed an elbow into Lansdale's chest, knocking the man backward as air whooshed from his chest. As Tom tried to turn and push Santa Romana away, just as quickly, Santa Romana twisted Tom's hand into an aikido hand lock and drove him to the ground. Lansdale jumped on his legs.

"Now, then," Santa Romana said. "We just want to give you a little something to cure your headache. In fact, you'll soon forget you've ever had a headache."

"Let me go!" Tom writhed against the man, but when Santa Romana again pressured Tom's arm, pain shot up Tom's neck, and he immediately submitted.

Tao wasted no time. Without even removing Tom's jacket, he jammed the needle into Tom's arm and pressed the plunger. Then Tao said, "There...He'll have a real nice trip."

"The truth is," Santa Romana said, releasing his grip on Tom, "you'll soon forget you've ever met me. That's a shame, too, since I was beginning to like you." Santa Romana dusted his hands together, as if wiping Tom from his life. "You'll forget you've been in the Philippines, for that matter." He looked at Tom, then at Lansdale, and smiled.

Lansdale allowed himself a small, tight smile as he massaged his ribs where Tom had elbowed him. "Don't worry, Warren, you asshole. You'll have new memories. Better ones. Pleasant memories. And we won't let you forget about the Philippines. We'll just . . . *rearrange* what you know about your stay on the islands." He snickered.

Nausea churned in Tom's stomach, and for a moment, he thought he'd vomit. Then, just as he was sure he would, his aching muscles relaxed. Thunder growled as the storm crept closer, but the rumbling soothed Tom. The darkening sky around him took on a soft, peach haze, and the rolling storm clouds no longer looked ominous, but curling and lovely. And the wind carried with it an exotic fragrance that filled his senses.

It smelled like Isabella.

"Izzy," he said, his voice singsong and soft. "Isabella."

Lansdale peered closely at him. "What did you say?"

"I . . . . I don't know. I'm burning up." Tom looked at the strange man whose eyeglasses reflected the melting sky above.

Tom chuckled. The sky was melting. The sky was melting. Rolls of color and flashes of brilliant light—light so intense it pricked his skin. It was lovely. Intriguing. He opened his arms wide and embraced this strange new world.

THE END

www.ingramcontent.com/pod-product-compliance
Lightning Source LLC
Chambersburg PA
CBHW051509170626
46811CB00002B/723